The Dark Lant
Tales

By

Lyn Watts

A collection of short stories

First Published July 2016

10 9 8 7 6 5 4 3 2 1 0

ISBN 978 0 993 2977 1 7

Published by Wattnott Publishing, Testers, Whatlington, Battle, TN33 0NS England

The Dark Lantern and Other Tales

CONTENTS

Foreword:

Lyn Watts worked in the National Health Service for 40 years. During this time she became experienced in most branches of nursing, eventually specialising in resuscitation and Life Support training. When she retired in 2014, she and her husband (also an NHS retiree) set up their own company, providing the same high-standard training to doctors, dentists and other healthcare professionals.

Lyn's work keeps her very busy, and most of her spare time is spent with her family, including her six young grandchildren, and with her beloved horse and dogs. However, she somehow still finds time to write!

This is Lyn's second book of short stories. Her first, "Traders of The Fifth Continent –Tales of Smugglers and Rascals on Romney Marsh" published in March 2015, was set in late Georgian times. This new book contains stories on a variety of themes, with several of them set in this same area, reflecting her interest in, and love of, the Marsh and its many historic churches. They are set in many different ages too. As with Lyn's first book, a few of the tales also contain elements of the supernatural! Some stories have already appeared in local magazines, but several are new.

The stories in this book are mainly fiction, products of Lyn's fertile imagination - although some are based on real events and people. "A Call to Arms" and "Hero's Return" even draw on events within our own family during World War Two, as recalled by our late parents (Lyn is my sister).

Carole Verrall M.B.E.
Norfolk, April 2016

Introduction

This is the second book of short stories from Lyn Watts. Some of the stories were written about fictitious events in the Romney Marsh in Kent, where her first stories were originally published. Most of the tales were actually written in the West Country where there is a little more peace and quiet than Sussex and the busy daily working life she leads. In Somerset the loudest sounds are the crows and jackdaws with the occasional dog bark.

The inspiration comes from all quarters. Some stories are deliberately misleading and have a quirky twist whilst some have distinctly ghostly tinges. There are three stories featuring Will and Graham - two country policemen. Others will surely follow in this series so look out for them.

Lyn's research work is as important to her as the writings themselves and she tries to get the background facts as accurate as possible in all her tales. She is widely read and the library at home has now extended into the loft. At the last count there were eleven bookcases in the house. The internet also provides valuable data and is an invaluable tool for any author. Lyn also has a wide experience of life. She has lived in Kent, London, Sussex and Somerset and has encountered people from all walks of life. Some have provided characters for her stories (mostly unwittingly!).

Stories continue to be written, so there will undoubtedly be further volumes to look forward to in the future. She is still being published regularly in magazines and enjoys the challenge of writing to a word count (usually very small) and then expanding those same stories for a wider, and less restricted, readership. I have had enormous pleasure in proof reading and editing these, and other, stories over the years. I hope you, the reader, will enjoy them as much as I have.

Charlie Watts. East Sussex April 2016

Emma's Tale

It was gathering dusk. The howling wind was blowing the torrential rain sideways into her face and taking her breath away. Not that she had much breath in the first place! The rain had plastered her hair to her head, and was dripping cold rivulets of water inside the collar of her inadequate lightweight coat. That didn't really make an awful lot of difference since she was already soaked to the skin.

She usually loved the marshes. That was the reason she had started out for a walk today, to take a last long look at them before she..."Well, no matter. Everything is pointless now anyway." She thought to herself. Something died within her when Ian died. He was only forty-five, it was so unfair. She had sacrificed having children and thrown everything into the business they had run together. He, being five years older than she, didn't mind quite so much, while her biological clock ticked fruitlessly away. She was comforted only by the thought that, when Ian reached fifty, they would sell up, retire and have the life of Reilly together travelling the world. This, of course, was before the cruel cancer had claimed him. The love of her life, all she had in the world, companion, husband, but, sadly, not father. No children. Nothing left of their love, and nothing to live for.

After the funeral, she had sold the business to a rival company who snapped it up for a substantial sum, and she had accepted an offer on the house that very morning. She told her friends that she might travel after all, now that she was a woman of considerable means. Unbeknown to them, she had saved the last of Ian's morphine and kept back all her prescribed sleeping pills and anti-depressants from the doctor. After this final look at her beloved marshes, she would go home, put on their favourite tune and wash the whole lot down with a bottle of Merlot. Blissful, permanent oblivion!

Now she cursed as she battled against the elements. She felt she had no energy. She had not eaten properly for weeks, whilst caring for Ian. She had hardly slept, and suddenly felt weak with exhaustion against the onslaught of the weather. Her one goal was to reach the little 13th century church of St Augustin's on the marsh. She could see it from here, and prayed that it was unlocked so that she could shelter and try to dry out a little, since she was feeling quite faint. A turn of the cold metal handle, a shoulder against and one final push of the heavy door – thank heaven it was unlocked and swung open to admit her. She'd never been inside this church before and was struck by the heavy silence, so thick it almost hurt her head. There was a strong smell of mouldering hymn books and damp wood, but to her surprise and delight, the whole interior was lit up with candles. She did not have too long to savour this as the ringing in her ears grew louder, black spots danced before her eyes and she slid gently onto her knees before collapsing forward in a dead faint.

She awoke to a familiar manly smell in her nostrils; a smell that caused a lump in her throat and a knot in her stomach. The smell was of shaving soap and linen, and reminded her of Ian. Opening her eyes, she found herself gazing into the kindest, softest hazel eyes. They were looking at her with some concern. They belonged to an attractive face, framed by thick, wavy, almost blue-black hair. Strong arms were cradling her shoulders, whilst a small silver hip flask was placed between her lips.

"You are quite safe", said a strong clear voice, "It's only brandy."

"Brandy for the parson..." she thought of the old smuggler's tale from the marshes – "watch the wall, my darling, while the gentlemen go by...."

Indeed, when she opened her eyes fully, it was a parson who was holding her.

"Come, madam, let us get you sat more comfortably." He helped her onto the nearest pew and placed her feet on a hassock. "Now you can get your breath back." He said, smiling.

With a flourish, he whipped his long black cloak off his own back and wrapped it around her, whilst offering more brandy.

"I'm George Benson, vicar of this parish. You're quite safe now."

"Thank you." She said, "I got caught by the storm on the marshes and just needed a little rest. I'll not trouble you for long."

"No trouble at all." He said.

She noticed the corners of his eyes crinkling in a most charming way. "The marshes are too exposed to be out for long in this sort of weather. You need some of the weather I've just left behind in Africa. It's too hot there at times."

As she rested back and relaxed he told her of his recent visit to Africa to formally open the St Augustin's Home for Orphans and Foundlings. He had raised the money to fund this, and was clearly very proud of his achievement. Secretly she though it a rather old fashioned name, but, then, he had rather old fashioned manners. A real gentleman clergyman. She found him enchanting. He went on to tell her about the poverty and the primitive conditions in Africa; the high infant and child death rate before St Augustin's gave them the chance of life.

"They always need funds." He said. "It is my life's work to keep it going. I intend to move out there and start a school when I retire from this parish."

As he spoke she felt herself relax. His arm was still around her shoulders and she felt safe and warm. His voice was soft and soporific, and, as the brandy did its work, her head slowly leaned on his shoulder so that she closed her eyes and drifted into sleep.

She awoke as the church flooded with light. Electric light! Brighter than before, the atmosphere was lighter and there was no longer the smell of damp hymn books in her nostrils.

"Gosh, sorry to disturb you, I didn't see you in the gloom." The words came from a jolly-hockey-sticks-gels type of voice. "I'm Cathy Grainger, vicar. Are you okay?"

She was a plumpish, but pleasant looking lady in her forties, with a shiny face and a mop of dark curly hair. She was smiling, but looked a little concerned.

"Sorry," said Emma, "I was walking on the marshes, got caught in the storm, and felt rather faint. Your colleague kindly let me rest here and was telling me all about St Augustin's in Africa."

She felt chilly now and noticed the warm cloak was no longer covering her. Cathy Grainger looked puzzled – colleague? Well, no matter, she thought.

Aloud she said "Yes, the mission school. So sad. If we do not meet our fundraising target it will have to close by Christmas -tragic after all of this time."

Now it was Emma's turn to look puzzled. "All this time? I thought it had only just opened."

"No, my dear, it's over 130 years old. It still survives, and we've had to modernise over the years, but it still retains the philosophy of its original founder."

Cathy continued talking, but Emma was no longer listening. She was heading for the door, her mind buzzing with ideas. To the right of the doorway was a wooden board listing all the past incumbents of St Augustin's. One name leapt out at her. The Rev. George H. Benson 1855 -1875. Emma spun on her heel and, pointing at the name, she asked Cathy "Wasn't he the founder of the orphanage?"

"Yes" said Cathy "although these days it's a school and not solely for orphans. He was a great person and a wonderful parish priest by all accounts - generous, kind and loved by his parishioners. Sadly he had a tragic end. He caught a fatal dose of pneumonia after bring caught in a severe storm on the marshes. He was only forty-five."

Now Emma knew what she had to do. Although the lump in her throat was almost too big to swallow and her eyes were pricking with tears, she felt peace and a quiet joy for the first time in months. She took Cathy's contact details, promising to be in touch. She went home to destroy her drug stash and begin packing for her trip to Africa. She had a purpose in life at last.

Gentleman's Relish

He felt guilty as he ended the call. This was the second time this month that he had rung in to the office feigning a "sickie". "A relapse of the earlier virus," he had claimed. "Feeling feverish." Well, that part was true, at any rate. He always felt slightly feverish at the thought of seeing her.

He had left home at the usual time this morning, so his long-suffering wife had no idea that he was not in work. "She'd hit the roof if she knew," he thought to himself. It's not as though he could have done anything to stop it. He was in the grip of the most powerful drug known to man. He had tried to resist, Lord knows he really had tried so hard, but she had cast a spell over him and he was powerless to her call. No, he simply could not keep away from her.

The very first time he saw her he was under her spell; the way she moved, her big liquid eyes, the soft golden colouring. She seemed to him to have a litheness about her, yet a spring in her step. And he loved her gracefully long legs.

He had fallen into the trap quite by chance. He had noticed her superficially and been surprised at how pleased he felt when he saw her for a second time. And then he couldn't get her out of his mind. She certainly knew how to impress (obviously learned from a man with far greater experience than he could ever hope to have).

Sometimes she teased him. She would not come up with the goods on every occasion. She let him down from time to time. She would coax him right to the edge only to disappoint at the last second. But still he came back for more. He knew he shouldn't. And yet, when she delivered it set his pulses racing, and the blood in his veins afire, so powerful were her charms.

He had saved up for this day. He kept a separate bank account and put a little aside from time to time just for these special occasions. His wife must never know. She might be suspicious, but she could prove nothing. Perhaps it was just a matter of time, he would have to take extra precautions.

He had vowed never to meet her again on the numerous times she had failed to deliver. "That's it," he'd say, "No more; never again." But, she had got to him. She was under his skin and, no matter how he tried, her pull was always there and it was too strong for him. "It can't last." He'd tell himself. Sooner or later his boss, or, worse, his wife, would find out. But this faded into insignificance whenever he saw her.

He drove east across the marshes, hardly noticing the plovers and the position of the sun, his mind was filled all with her. Then, at last, he was there. He parked the car and walked the last few hundred yards. He could lose himself in the throng of people around him - a fair old bustle in the brightness of the afternoon's sunshine. There was noise everywhere and he couldn't see her at first. His heart skipped a beat. There she was; tall, elegant, fit – his darling golden girl. What would be his fate today? Would she just tease him, play with his emotions or would she come good today? He told himself it did not matter, but, of course, it did!

He caught her eye and smiled. She gave him a knowing look and he could have sworn that she winked at him. For a while she was gone from his sight and then he thought he could see her again in the melee. He caught his breath. He was beginning to get excited. His throat tightened, he felt himself trembling slightly, although it was not a cold day. His fingernails dug into his palms. And now she was running towards him. Yes, she was definitely running towards him. He could stand it no longer. He closed his eyes. When he opened them again she had run past him. He could not believe it. She was ten lengths clear of the field. She'd certainly come good this time around. His beautiful golden girl, Gentleman's Relish, had won the 2.30 at Folkestone, and this time she was 33-1.

A Call to Arms

"NO, NO, NO, OH Come ON!" She cried, exasperated at them. Her Baton tapped an irritable tattoo on the music stand. "It's meant to be FORTE!"

"Forty? Sounds more like an 'undred." Muttered Fred in the front row, his neighbour George sniggered.

"Then it becomes moderate." She continued "Andante!"

"Dante?" Ernie said to Cyril next to him, "Didn't he have an Inferno?"

"Infernal more like!" said Cyril, "This blasted Palestrina early music malarkey is infernal, can't we have a decent English Onward Christian Soldiers or Fight the Good Fight instead?"

"Please, PLEASE!" she cried, really frustrated with them now. "We MUST get on. Time is really short if we are to perform this at Evensong on Sunday."

She sometimes wished that she hadn't taken them on. The St Mary's choir, such as was left of it, was her bit for the war effort, when she wasn't on fire warden's duty, or running the little St Mary's Church of England Primary school, her day job. Mr Steele, the headmaster and choirmaster, was now in Trichinopoly with his RAF squadron. In fact, most of the younger members of the choir were absent. The young ladies nursing or working the land and the young men abroad, many of them had gone to Canterbury and signed up with the 'Buffs' - The Royal East Kent regiment to give it it's full name - and were posted to far flung, dangerous places like Tripoli, Malta or North Africa. All except poor Gordon, a big, ponderous, slightly slow-witted young man with flat feet and adenoids. Delicate, as his mother described all 6'4" of him. Gordon was the strongest physically and was also their strongest Tenor, which said a lot for the general standard of the other singers.

These were, however, dire times when needs must and at least it maintained some semblance of normality in their otherwise topsy- turvey village life, and somewhat male-depleted Church services.

"Let's take it from the A minor, 3rd Bar in – Thank you Mrs Pumfrey!" A nod to the organist and they were off again.

A maddening lot, especially the men; they clearly found it strange to be led by a woman, and a youngish one at that. Celia was only 29 years old, but she was an accomplished musician. Mr Steele was fighting for King and Country and, besides, no one else wanted to take on the task.

"Better! Not bad!" She said "Not bad at all this time through. Alright, we'll leave it there for tonight; see you all for the final practice Saturday morn ..." But she was cut short by the running footsteps and breathless apology of Will Carlton, the village policeman.

"I'm so sorry to interrupt you, Miss Meakin," He said, "but we need Major Rogers to mobilize his men! Jerry has just been spotted bailing out of a plane over Bennett's bottom field."

Major Rogers was in charge of the Local Defence Volunteers or the Homeguard, as they were known. Will Carlton looked flushed and panicked and was clearly very out of breath.

"What do you mean man? Jerry's bailed out?"

Theo Rogers was a stout, florid man with a large ginger moustache, puce complexion and a short temper. He fixed his watery blue eyes on Will Carlton and puffed out his chest as though waiting for a written explanation.

"Just that, Major Rogers, Sir!" Quavered Will, "Plane went over, Heinkel I think it were. Me and old Ted Burton saw a parachute floating down into Bennett's field, but the plane kept going, like, we didn't hear no sound of crash, so we reckoned it musta ditched into the sea, musta had a fault or summit and the pilot decided to bail out."

"I see." Said Theo Rogers, suddenly assuming a military air. He was a veteran of Paschendale (and likely Rourkes Drift too if half the village gossip about his age was to be believed!) He now took command of the LDV's and sometimes, the village in general.

"Right men, now listen to me! Get moving! We must mobilise. Grab anything you have to hand. Vicar, VICAR!"

"Yes, Mr Rogers, coming!" Poor Reverend Moseby had come out of retirement to serve St Mary's while the regular incumbent, George Peters, was serving as Army Chaplain to the 5th Battalion of The Buffs in North

Africa. "What can I do to help?" He asked in a feeble, cracked voice.

"Key to the sexton's shed! Quick, man!" said Major Rogers.

"Ooooh!" Said Mrs Winters, "My Eric's home on leave from the Navy. Shall I run over 'ome and get 'im?"

"Ooooh! So is my Bert" said Mrs Jarman. "He can get orff his backside and give you an 'and!"

Celia found it reassuring that at least two able bodied, youngish professional men would be present to assist the bumbling brigade of granddads.

Major Rogers had unlocked the sexton's shed and was busy distributing shovels, rakes, hoes and shears to the men. Eric Winters had arrived with an iron poker and Bert Jarman ran in wielding his cricket bat (he could run too, and had scored the odd century or two for the local team in his day.)

Celia began to feel alarmed. "Please be careful." She pleaded.

"Don't worry, Miss Meakin, we'll be fine." Said Eric Winter, in a soothing voice.

"Not you lot," said Celia, "The German Pilot!" She thought of her own brother, Tom, not yet twenty, and in the RAF stationed at Biggin Hill.

"He is probably only young and will be very scared. He may well be injured. He will no doubt be very relieved to rest up in a British Prisoner of War camp for the rest of the duration and won't need you lot offering violence and scaring him half to death."

"Now then, men!" Blustered Theo Rogers. "Stealth is the name of the game. Be like dad, keep mum!"

Looking pleased with himself, he held a tobacco stained finger up to his lips. "No stomping in your size 13's Gordon, we will crawl up the side of the mound on our bellies so he doesn't see us coming. When we have a good view of the whole field we will spread out across the headland, then, at my command, like this," - he waved an arm in a sharp downward movement, - "we will rush down upon him and take him by surprise. Watch out though, he may be armed. Stealth is our masterstroke. Softly, softly catchee monkee!"

He looked very pleased with himself, but Celia thought how ridiculous he sounded. All this trouble for one poor, very probably terrified and homesick young man, but, she supposed, he was the enemy after all.

"Right Men!" Continued Theo Rogers. "Let's go, and good luck!"

As they marched off, looking a real rag-bag lot, Celia and the other women watched them with mixed feelings. They opened up the church hall and the atmosphere was very tense as they waited. Reverend Moseby was quietly praying. Mrs Jarman was pacing up and down with her arms folded and smoking a Woodbine. Mrs Winter had busied herself in the kitchen setting out teacups – having first switched on the urn.

"They'll all need tea when they bring him back won't they?" She said, to reassure herself more than anyone else.

Much to Celia's irritation, Mrs Pumfrey had opened the hall's piano and was playing the odd note which made Celia feel like she was losing her mind. She tried to work out whether the choir were up to performing Mozart's Ave Verum at the Blackwell girl's wedding and decided they had better practice from now onwards. Nobody said very much at all. The Urn hissed as only urns can. The piano keys plonked; the Vicar's prayers sounded as a low mutter. All of a sudden there came an almighty explosion which shook the ground and set the tea cups and rafters rattling!

It was Celia who first heard them approaching, Bert Jarman was using language that would have caused blushes on the Fo'csle deck of a whaling boat while Gordon was laughing hysterically. They ran to the doors to meet them. All the men were caked in mud and dust, with black hands and faces and hair all awry. Most of them had their jackets off and had filled them with something bulky, Celia couldn't see what.

"Inside, inside quick!" Cried Eric Winter. "Edie, where's that tea?"

While the ladies served tea, Bert Jarman explained. "We were following orders from Attila an' we got about 'arfway up Burrow Hill on our bellies - couldn't see the field, Jerry or nuffink being as 'ow we was on our bellies, see! All of a sudden there was this almighty bang. Fair shook us up, I can say! Me ears are still hissing from it! Next thing you know, we gets showered in mud and bloody spuds – 'scuse my French, Miss (to Celia.) It was only a blasted parachute mine, not Jerry at all! Trust Bennett to have a field planted full of potatoes!"

The men started laughing and revealed the stash of potatoes collected in their jackets.

"Mother fetch a sack from the cupboard!" Said Bert Jarman. "We can all 'ave roast spuds for a six-month now!"

Pacemaker

Hello there, come a little closer. What am I doing? Well top stable jockey or not I still have to take a turn with the mucking out of the stables around here, and the horses won't feed themselves now will they? Who am I? My name is Finbar Grady and I don't mind telling yer, I'm rather pleased with meself at the moment. I only went and rode the winner of the 2000 guineas this year, making me mammy proud and ensuring me place as top stable Jockey on our yard here in Newmarket. Mind you, I still think me and Brewie, that's the horse, we had a little help. But let me start at the beginning.

I'm not from Newmarket, No, I was born in Kildare and was sent to Jockey school here by my parents, when I was 16 years old. Now I'm not very tall but it is a struggle to keep me weight down enough to ride the lightweights and I was, how shall I say, mediocre at best so I thought meself lucky when I was offered to join Mr Wentworth here in Hamilton Stud Lane. He is a good trainer and a fair man. I worked hard and got to ride in some of the lesser races, but usually the rank outsiders.

Now the 2000 guineas is for 3 year olds only and Brew Ha Ha, or Brewie to his mates was not high in the Bookies reckoning - quoted at 33-1 best odds - but I didn't care; it was one of the biggest races I had ever ridden in.

For some time I had caught a glimpse now and then of a lovely grey horse in the lane, ridden by a morose looking, very tall, jockey a few years older than me.

Every time I went to get a closer look or to speak to them they had gone and no one knew which yard they came from. I had put them quite out of my mind until the night before the race.

I had been fasting all day and spent hours at the sauna to make the weight needed, coming home to an early night I though it odd that in the twilight the man on the grey was riding down the lane. I didn't see where they went as I turned in almost immediately and went up to me bed.

I didn't sleep much - too excited about the race. Me Mammy and Dad were coming over to watch it and were going to stay in the area for a couple of days. After a fitful few hours of dozing, it was time to get up and get meself and Brewie ready. I had other duties to perform first and other horses to get ready for me more senior colleagues to ride, but finally it was time to get Brewie ready and get meself to the weighing room. To my relief I made the weight with no penalties and finally we were lined up in the stalls.

I usually get a little nervous at this point but today I could hardly breathe. Me throat was dry and me jaw was aching from clenching me teeth with nerves, I didn't expect to be in the placings but I just wanted to give a good safe ride for meself and dear Brewie, as I was quite fond of him.

At last the flag was down, the stalls opened and we were off. I always felt better once we started and today was no exception, Mr Wentworth had told me to hang back at first then push him on for the final three furlongs, but Brewie was on a roll. He was really going some right from the start. Then I noticed him. The tall guy with the sad face on the grey; he was just ahead of us at me right elbow. At first I thought it was me mate Derry on Sambuca but no, it was this guy from Hamilton Lane. He was wearing very odd silks, a bit old fashioned but he was a great pacemaker for Brewie who determined to keep up with the grey. We passed the marker for the last three furlongs, but I didn't need to push him on, we ran clear of the field just behind the rear of the grey. I was ecstatic thinking to meself that we would be in second place at 33-1, then we were past the post and I released me reins patting his neck looking to see how far behind the winner we were, but to my amazement, the grey was nowhere to be seen.

The next hour was a blur, Mr Wentworth was so delighted he hugged me, and so did Brewie's owners! I tried to explain to them that they grey was first. Had he fallen and I hadn't noticed I wondered? But they all ignored that. I began to think I was imagining things.

We were taken - me, Mammy and Dad for several drinks in the Trainers and Owners bar. I hadn't been in here before, having never ridden a winner for such an important race. On the wall were several paintings of past winners. One of them was of the tall thin jockey that rode the grey.

"There" I said, "that's the rider I was telling you about!"

Mr Wentworth looked serious and suddenly sober for a minute.

"That's Fred Archer, son." He said quietly. "He was an English jockey here in the last quarter of the nineteenth century. He won the 2000 Guineas four times and was the most successful Jockey of his day but he shot himself in 1886 in a fit of depression after the death of his wife. His favourite horse was a grey!"

Well, I don't know much about many things but I do know that I owe my good fortune to that tall guy with the sad face, He was the pacemaker for dear old Brewie and thanks to him, Brewie has a good career ahead of him as a stud and my career has taken off. Well now, would ya look at the toime, I need to get finished, another big race tomorrow, and this toime I'm ridin' the favourite.

Te Deum

Anne felt some fear and trepidation. Despite this, she felt excitement. What lay ahead for her? This sacrifice was what her whole life had worked towards. This was her ultimate gift to God. She had been the anchoress at St Dunstan's for the past ten years. The approval from the bishop for her enclosure had come when she was a mere sixteen. A little cell, just eight foot by six had been constructed against the south aisle of the church. The outer grill, through which she would receive all the provisions vital to existence, had a view of the south side of the churchyard and fields beyond. On the inner wall the little squint looked onto the altar and chancel to enable her to take part in the services.

Whilst giving their permission, her parents were concerned that she may go insane, or even die from boredom. She found, however, that the daily devotions took around four hours of the day; then she took part in all of the services – following them through the squint. There was also time for her personal prayers and devotional readings, as well as interventions on behalf of the villagers. These same people, along with her family and kind friends, brought all her food, drinks and daily needs and placed them through the grating on the outer wall.

Anne had been blessed with a most beautiful singing voice and was also an accomplished musician. St Dunstan's was approaching its 300th anniversary. There was to be a huge thanksgiving service and the bishop was reported to be coming. Father Thomas had charged her with writing a Te Deum for St Dunstan's, to be performed at the service with herself as cantor accompanied by the monks.

Once she had completed the piece, she and the monks had practiced until it was nearly perfect. Now it would be ready for performance at the service on Sunday. Although slightly nervous at the thought of her work being performed publicly, she was really looking forward to it. But that was before.

*****

The King had virtually declared war on the holy Church of Rome. He was the second of these Tudors, another Henry. He had caused a huge schism within the church since he had seen fit to declare himself head of the Church in England; all this, apparently, because he had been captivated by a protestant strumpet, whom he had married and then beheaded just three years later.

And so it came about that two years after the execution any monasteries which had escaped the initial destruction which the King had had ordered, were being persecuted relentlessly by Thomas Cromwell, his puppet. Even now Cromwell's henchmen were on their way to destroy St Dunstan's and the monk's home. Father Thomas had told her to flee. "Come while you still can," he had said "The Bishop will understand. We cannot guarantee your safety." But she was answerable to one even higher than Father Thomas and a hundred Bishops. This was not all about her physical safety; it was about her promise to God and the safety of her soul.

"I will stay here, and face whatever the future might hold." She declared.

She was alone in her cell. She waited and prayed. She was afraid, yet was, strangely, at peace. Whatever happened, though, she must save her musical manuscript.

From the grating she could see horsemen riding fast across the marshes. They would be upon her within minutes. Father Thomas had broken the Bishop's seal and opened her cell before leaving himself. Grabbing the manuscript, she wrapped it in her spare wimple, and left her cell for the first time in ten years. There was a loose tile by the altar steps. She had seen it before. Carefully, but quickly, she prised it up. She was able to push the manuscript out of sight and as far as she could reach. The tile was speedily replaced and she fled back to her cell to wait and pray.

*****

The 700th anniversary of St Dunstan's was a mere two weeks away. Luke was really panicking now. He was the chief chorister, and his greatest ambition was to win a place at King's, Canterbury next year when he would be thirteen. The previous year St Dunstan's was finally brought into the 20th century when it became electrified. Well, it was 1937, after all. This did, however, necessitate laying cables beneath the floor of the nave and chancel. The space beneath the altar steps was being dug out when an ancient manuscript was discovered. It was wrapped in some sort of yellowing calico. There was much excitement when it was revealed to be a piece of music – a Te Deum for St Dunstan's written in Latin. The hand seemed to indicate a date around early to mid-1500s. It was not signed, but it did coincide with the period of history when St Dunstan's had its own anchorite or anchoress. The antiquarians believed it had been hidden deliberately to avoid destruction in the time of the dissolution.

The Bishop had decided that it would be fitting to perform the work for the first time in 400 years at the thanksgiving service for the 700th anniversary of St Dunstan's. Luke was to be cantor. If the Bishop approved of his singing, it was likely that the deanery would sponsor his place at King's.

The boy's nerves were getting the better of him, and the performance was getting nearer and nearer. He seemed to be fine when practicing with Mr Swale, the choirmaster, but, in front of his parents, his fellow choristers and even the vicar his throat would tighten and sometimes a barely audible croak would come out.

"Practice, practice, practice!" shouted Mr Swale, in desperation. And so Luke had done just that. But he still felt apprehension and tension when performing the piece in front of an audience.

"Go into the church on your own and go over it again and again until you are confident of it." Mr Swale was determined to settle his nerves.

Luke did this for an hour after school every day. At first Luke thought he had imagined it; a stronger, richer voice accompanying him. He thought it must be the echo of an empty church. Then one evening he believed he caught a glimpse of a thin white face appearing briefly in the small squint set in the side of the Sheldon chapel in the south aisle. He could not be sure. It had been a momentary flash before his eye and then it was gone. He felt a little afraid. This was reputed to be where the ancient anchorite cell had been before it was destroyed in 1538. The Sheldon family had built their fine chapel in 1620, but let the surviving squint remain so as to have a better view of the altar.

Next evening Luke noticed that the voice was even stronger. So was his impression of the face at the squint. Although pale, he had the impression of great beauty and she seemed to be wearing something resembling a veil and wimple. But when he turned to look, the impression vanished and so did the voice.

At school he asked his history teacher about St Dunstan's. It had, apparently, been one of the last churches to have an anchoress. She had been Ann Dereham. Little was known about her fate, but it was believed that she had fallen foul of Thomas Cromwell's men in the 1530s.

Now that he had a probable candidate, Luke allowed himself to relax more in her company. He still sensed, rather than saw, her presence. Each time he sang the piece he became aware of a voice leading him. His confidence grew. Finally, one evening, he was sure he had seen her full face on. She was looking through the squint; a small lady – very beautiful with dark, sad, eyes. He did not feel the need to talk to her, afraid that, if he did so, the spell might be broken forever.

The next time he performed the Te Deum for Mr Swale and the choir she was singing with him - out of his sight, but with her voice as strong and as sweet as ever. He then gained the confidence to sing solely from his heart and with all the power and grace he possessed.

"Fantastic, my boy!" exclaimed a beaming Mr Swale, "Sing like that on Sunday and you'll win them all. His grace included! Your practice has paid off."

Luke prayed that she would be with him on Sunday. He felt that he couldn't cope if she deserted him. At the final practice on the Saturday she was at the squint watching him the whole time he sang. When he had finished he thought he saw her raise a hand to him and then he knew that she would be there for the special performance.

Sunday morning found Luke very excited and quietly confident. He guessed that he was the only one who could see her, but he knew that he could hide behind her lovely strong voice. She would carry them through.

The robed choir filed slowly down the aisle as Mr Swale gave the tonic sol fa on the organ. Luke began to sing the cantor part of the Te Deum.

Not only could he hear her, but she was walking next to him. She was slight - not much taller than him - pale, thin; gowned and wearing veil and wimple. She was very beautiful and this time he noticed her eyes were smiling. She looked really happy. Luke felt very honoured to be singing this piece of music and he was sure she had written it. He opened his lungs and sang from the heart. He was superb.

The music finished and all fell silent. Luke saw her slip into the Sheldon chapel. Her face appeared at the squint. She smiled broadly at him. Then she was gone.

As the service ended Mr Swale approached Luke. He had a beam from ear to ear. "Well done, lad, you'd best be buying books. His grace has agreed to sponsor your place at Kings. You were wonderful."

"But, it was the anchoress," thought Luke to himself.

Aloud he said: "Thank you, sir, I hope I did justice to the Te Deum."

September arrived. Luke was all packed and ready to leave for the start of term at Kings. Before leaving he went alone to the Sheldon chapel. Leaving a single white rose below the squint he whispered "Thank you." Then he left to find what lay ahead.

A Martello Mystery

"But Sarg, I think I AM ready for the sergeants exams." Exclaimed Will. "I'm ready for a bigger challenge and some responsibility now, I'm sure I can pass them."

Will Simmons was a young Constable in the Kent Constabulary based in the villages around Hythe and Dymchurch. Since his de-mob from the army in 1945, he had been content to live a quiet uneventful life, cycling from village to village investigating Mrs Thompson's stolen eggs or helping to find Granny Barnes lost cat. Now, after two years of this, he was getting bored. He had recovered from the terrible scare Hitler had given to him (and the rest of Europe) and was ready for something a little more challenging. He had been successful in the Army, rising to the rank of Corporal. Now, when anything exciting hove into view, he was left minding the fort whilst his Guvnor and the other lads got the action. Just last week, Graham, his oppo, had helped to catch the Burmarsh sheep rustlers. Will was missing out.

"Bide your time, lad." Said kindly Sergeant Watson, "You've enough years ahead for that... Oh no! Not that dratted child again!"

The dratted child Sergeant Watson was referring to was little Nancy (Nan) Burrows – a scruffy six year old urchin with a mass of unruly dark curls, a permanently dirty face and a cheeky gap-toothed grin. She got bored waiting around for her ne'er-do-well father to finish drinking at the local pub, so would drift over to the police station. Sometimes, if Sergeant Watson wasn't looking, Will and Graham would give her peppermints and a glass of orange squash. If they weren't around Sergeant Watson would give her most of his lunchtime sandwiches and a shiny sixpence telling her to hide it from her father! He felt sorry for her and tried to put a little joy into her dreary life.

"Dad's in the boozer ag'in!" said Nan. "He's no work on today, so can't pay Mrs Kemp to 'ave me for the day. Got anyfink for me to do?"

John Burrows was a shifty scoundrel who was often on the wrong side of the law but was good at covering his tracks. He was involved in all sorts of shady deals - sheep stealing being one of them. When Nancy was just two years old, his poor wife had escaped the beatings by dying of tuberculosis. He was left with the child to raise on his own. As an itinerant farm labourer he was known to be a lazy drunkard. Because of Nan he was unable to work away from home. This meant there was often no work for him. That was when he turned to poaching and petty crime to keep himself in beer. When in work, he paid Mrs Kemp - a slovenly, local baby farmer - to mind Nan after school; but when there was no work, the poor child had to fend for herself, following him around. It was little wonder that she often skipped school. She had a fascination for the local bobbies and was as fond of the police station as her father hated it.

Some weeks later Will was shopping in Hythe on his day off. He happened to pass the pawnbroker's shop and spotted a scruffy child's threadbare coat and a small pair of worn boots in the window. They looked, to him, like Nancy's. Now he came to think of it, he hadn't seen Nan Burrows for a week or two. An uneasy feeling crept over him. He walked into the shop.

"Morning, Mr Grover. Has John Burrows been hocking his daughter's clothes by any chance? "

"Well now, Constable Simmons, he did pop in last week. Said he had work away and the child was going to live with her grandmother in Rye. He reckoned she would get the girl some fine new boots and coat, so wouldn't be needing these ones." He pointed to the coat and boots in the shop window

Will thanked him, but felt uneasy about it. He said so to Sergeant Watson the next day at the station.

"That's easy, lad. Ask Old Mother Kemp when you're next passing her door."

Will did that later on the same day. Mrs Kemp hadn't seen Nan more than a fortnight.

"That useless layabout still owes me ten bob! Don't s'pose I'll ever see that again now Nan 'as gone to 'er grandma to live; an' all because he were too mean to pay me to 'ave 'er."

Will left feeling even more concerned. Sergeant Watson, however, was not in the least bit worried. He took things at face value. Will felt very uneasy. If she had gone to her grandmother's, she would need boots wouldn't she? He decided to cycle over to Rye on his next day off.

The following Saturday found him puffing into Rye on his bicycle. He knew where Nan's maternal grandmother lived. No, she hadn't seen hide nor hair of either Nan nor that useless lump since Christmas - when he had stolen a florin from her old jug on the mantle, the light fingered waste of space, was the gist of the conversation!

Having left the old lady still sounding off about that useless piece of lard, Will began to ask questions in the local pubs. There was honour amongst thieves, but none where John Burrows was concerned! Seems he was distrusted even amongst his own kind. Some local lads had been looking for 'lost Sheep' on the Marsh. (This was an old ruse used by sheep rustlers, who would steal and slaughter a sheep, then use a marker to show where they had hidden it for collection after dark.) These 'assistant shepherds' had found a piece of material which they thought marked a hiding hole. When they investigated they found part of a child's dress. One of them pulled it from his pocket (he was going to hand it in at the police station, but hadn't got round to it.) He passed it to Will. It looked like Nan's dress, and, suspiciously, it appeared to be damaged by fire.

That was enough to convince Sergeant Watson. A manhunt began for John Burgess. It was soon established that he had been seen about 10 days previously in Dymchurch, so that was the starting point. It took about four days but, by the Thursday, Sergeant Watson took a phone call. His face brightened:

"They've got 'im lad! " He said to Will.

Burrows had been found in Dover. He was hanging around the docks trying to find work on a boat as a means of getting to Calais. When brought back to the cells at Hythe Police Station he was smug and cocky. "Don't know!" was all he'd say when asked about Nancy. It was suggested that he had done away with her. "Well where's the body then?" Was his retort.

Will knew that without a body there was no proof with which to charge Burrows and he could walk free.

He couldn't get little Nan out of his head. He found himself dreaming about her. He had a recurring dream in which she was waving at him from the top window of a Martello Tower. It looked familiar but in his dream, every time he ran into the tower, she disappeared. This happened, several times a night. Sergeant Watson, very reasonably, pointed out to him that they could not search every single tower along the coast on the strength of a dream, so Will decided to make his own investigation. Dymchurch had been one of the last sightings of Burgess so Will started there. It was a complete waste of a day off. He knew he would recognise the dream tower, and it was none of the real ones he knew of. There followed some hectic days at work and, therefore, it was a few days later when he happened to be cycling along Hythe seafront that he spotted the exact tower of his dream. This particular one had been used as an observation post during the war to direct the cross channel shelling operations. It had stood empty and unused this past two years. As he looked the hairs rose on the back of his neck! There on the top floor at the window was Nancy Burrows! She was waving at him!

He forced his way into the tower calling her name all the while. But he soon discovered that she couldn't be on the top floor. The door to the stairway was padlocked and bolted securely. He looked around. Then he saw her behind him on the ramp to the lower basement. She smiled her familiar smile and ran down into the darkness. Will followed. His feet became wet. The lower basement was completely flooded and there was no sign of Nancy.

Back at the station Will had great trouble convincing Sergeant Watson to listen! Finally, after threatening to resign, he agreed to go along with Will to question Burrows.

"Did you put her in the Tower, Burrows? " He asked.

"Which trouble maker told you that?" Replied a cocky Burrows.

"Nancy did!" Hissed Will, his face a mere four inches from the father.

Burrows recoiled in horror. He said nothing, but the shock written on his face spoke for him.

They left him. Sergeant Watson said:

"Alright, lad, we'll arrange a search of the tower basement."

Will was granted permission to assist with the search. After some dredging and digging, a small bundle, wrapped in a tarpaulin, was found. Lifting it to drier ground, it was unwrapped. There lay the last pathetic mortal remains of little Nancy Burrows.

Gentle hands reverently took her out of the tower. Will felt sick and, yet, relieved. He was allowed to confront Burrows, with Sergeant Watson in attendance. The photographic evidence from the scene was conclusive and Burrows broke down.

"Since I'll swing now anyway, you may as well know the truth. I loved her, but she dragged me down. It cost me twelve bob a week to old Mother Kemp just to mind her while I worked. That was twelve bob less beer money!"

Will felt Sergeant Burrows hand restrain him before he could get his hands round Burrows throat! He consoled himself with the thought that the hang-man would soon finish the job, and he, for one, would shed no tears for him.

The community were wonderful. Everyone pulled together to give little Nan a decent Christian burial in the village churchyard. A fine headstone was erected inscribed "Nancy Burrows 1941 to 1947. Died in tragic circumstances"

Will made sure there were always fresh flowers on the grave.

The day after the execution of John Burrows, Sergeant Watson handed Will a form.

"What's this, then?" He enquired.

"It's the application form for your Sergeant's exams." Came the reply. "High time you moved up the ranks, my son."

A Hard Night at St Cuthbert's

Sally Bryant yawned and stretched, then draining the dregs of her coffee she stuck her knitting needles through her wool and stuffed the part knitted baby jacket into her knitting bag with the other coloured balls of wool. Sally was a staff nurse at St Cuthbert's hospital, one of the oldest hospitals in London. Built in the 1300's by monks to serve the poor sick of the city it was an ancient building with numerous corridors, nooks and crannies.

Usually on day duty on the Coronary Ward, Sally had been asked to swap onto nights for the week due to staff sickness. She was a little nervous in the old building at night, set around a square courtyard; all outer doors were locked at night obliging the staff to travel from wing to wing via the basement corridors. These were ancient, musty and the only lights were the dim night lights casting a greenish hue giving the impression of being in a semi dark cave.

To get from the Coronary wing to the staff canteen for her meal break Sally had to travel from one side of the square to the other via the basement corridor. Going to break wasn't too bad but coming back was eerie. Once in the canteen, the junior doctors used to entertain the nurses with stories and legends of the ancient hospital. It broke the boredom of reheated, microwaved, meals and tasteless coffee from the machine. Sally joined her friend, Katie, from Orthopaedics to eat their supper together. Soon they were joined by Dr Simon Diamond. He delighted in scaring the nurses and always seemed to have a new sensational story or spooky tale to tell.

Sally had finished eating and was on her second cup of strong black coffee when he started. Noting that Sally was knitting baby clothes for her sister, who was about to deliver her first child, he asked: had they heard the story of the ghostly Sister?

"Here we go." remarked Katie under her breath.

Without waiting for a reply from the girls, Simon Diamond began.

He told of a Sister Margaret at the hospital during the second war. She had the misfortune to fall truly and deeply in love with a man she had met at a tea dance. They saw each other twice weekly - on her night off and her half day. They spoke of marriage, but he enlisted as a fighter pilot in the RAF at the outbreak of hostilities. Before he went away they spent the night together. He bought her a modest ring and wrote to her regularly from his base in Kent.

The inevitable happened; his plane was hit by ground fire on his way back from a mission, he limped back to base but had to crash land. He was quite severely burnt before the ground crew could get him out of the cockpit. He was brought into St Cuthbert's and, strangely, to the very ward of his sweetheart. She nursed him most diligently, but he was morose and reluctant to talk to her. She put this down to shock and pain from his injuries, but after a couple of days he had visitors. A tall slim woman arrived to see him accompanied by a child of about 4 or 5 years. On being asked her identity she proclaimed herself to be his wife and the little girl his daughter!

Margaret gave no outward sign of shock or surprise at all; she showed the woman to his bedside and left them to it. After the visitors had left Margaret was doing the drug round before lights out and the patients settled for the night. She took her paramour his pain killers and sleeping pills. She had increased the dose 10 times! On her second hourly ward round she found him stiff and cold with blue lips, calmly pulling the sheets over his face, she opened the window. They were three floors up. She jumped to her death on the square below.

"They do say" continued Simon "that her poor shade stalks the corridors at night as a dark shadow, following other nurses to warn them against the same mistake, her penance for her guilt at what she had done."

"Poppycock!" said Katie "Gosh! Time I went back."

"Me too." said Sally, and, picking up her bag, she set off for her lonely walk under the square in the dark corridors to get back to the coronary wing. Her mind was filled with the tragic story of poor Sister Margaret. She had heard rumours of a suicide during the war years. Her ears detected a faint sound: 'Splat, swish swish, rattle rattle splat swish swish!'

The hairs on the back of her neck rose. She became acutely aware of the shadows, looking around she saw a dark shadowy blob bouncing along the corridor behind her. She felt her mouth dry up and her blood freeze. Quickening her pace, the blob quickened too. She could see the light at the end of the tunnel by the lifts, she started running, the blob kept up with her pace, bouncing crazily along behind her, at the same time the splat swishy noise grew louder, feeling as though her heart would burst she ran headlong towards the light then smack!

She ran straight into old Phil the night porter who was mopping the floor with soapy water Splat, the mop went then swish swish and finally rattle rattle in the metal bucket before the next Splat!

" 'ere 'ere steady on Nurse!" he exclaimed.

"Oh! Phil, thank God!" she began, but he cut her short

"Look 'ere, Staff!" he continued, "Your ball of wool is trailing along behind you, caught on your knitting bag, Good job it didn't unravel itself!"

Out of the Darkness

Maggie watched the countryside fly past in a blur from the train window. She felt relieved that she had taken this step, to see a psychiatrist about her problem. Well, one of her problems anyway. She fingered her cheek. It only hurt now when she pressed it lightly with her fingers, and the bruising had faded sufficiently to be hidden with a light application of foundation cream and blusher. Long sleeves hid the bruising on her arms where Roger had held her while screaming insults into her face, telling her how useless, unattractive and stupid she was. She must be, or else why did she manage to make him so angry. She had been inclined to agree with him about her stupidity, especially in view of her latest problem.

Maggie had moved in with Roger Bovie just over a year ago. He had been charming at first; handsome, well dressed and had made her feel special; that was until just after they moved in together. She then found out that he was an obsessive and a bully. His morning toast had to be cut just so and exactly the right amount of sugar in his coffee, almost to the last grain. If things weren't presented exactly as he wanted he would sulk at first, then, as the weeks went by, he turned from sulking to shouting insults and throwing crockery around.

Finally one day when he had a morning meeting to attend at work, her ironing of his white shirt did not live up to his exacting standards and he grabbed the hot iron and plunged it down on the back of her hand. He had stormed out leaving her crying over the sink, her hand under the running cold tap. When she had finally cooled and dressed the burn she found she was late for her own job.

She rushed into the flower shop where she worked, twenty minutes late using her burnt hand as the excuse but did not tell Anne, her friend and colleague, how she had managed to burn herself. Her tear stained face gave her away. As they made up wedding flowers together for a customer order, Anne broached the subject:

"Why do you stay with him?" she asked. "He is a control freak. He stops you seeing your friends; when was the last time your sister was allowed to visit you? Or me for that matter? He wants you to himself so that he can control and bully you!"

Now that it was out in the open, Maggie felt relieved. At least she could talk freely to Anne about things. Like the time she forgot to put sugar in his coffee and he emptied the cup over her head, or when she was late home and he gave her a backhander across the face causing the bruising that she was now able to disguise with makeup. She knew she should leave him but he made her believe that she was useless and that no one else would want her. She would be unable to manage alone, he had told her as much, and then there was the other, new problem.

It started after the incident with the iron, she went to the hall cupboard to get the ironing board out and found, to her horror, that she was seized with panic. A feeling of nausea and dizziness came over her and she had trouble going into the cupboard to get the things out. Anne said it was probably a sub-conscious reaction to the iron burn. Then it started to happen every time she went into a confined space. She found she had to take the stairs up to their second floor apartment as the lift sent her into a blind panic and she couldn't breathe. Going into any cupboard, even just putting her head into the larder to get the spices when cooking, caused her to have palpitations and she found herself shaking and gasping in fear.

Finally, when she found she couldn't shut the bathroom door at the shop without feeling that she was suffocating, she confessed to Anne who diagnosed claustrophobia and booked her the appointment with the London Doctor whom she was now travelling to meet.

Roger knew nothing about the appointment. Anne was her boss, and the owner of the flower shop, so Maggie was going in work time and would be home before Roger could realise she hadn't been working as usual. Anne was paying the fee also - which was just as well since the building in Wimpole Street where Dr Kressler had his consulting rooms, looked very salubrious.

Dr Kressler was a kind looking, quietly spoken man with a small grey beard, but very dark eyebrows. He listened attentively while she explained her problem. She purposely failed to mention Roger or their relationship at all.

"It may take a few consultations before we can get to the bottom of it." He warned Maggie "With your permission, I am going to try some hypnosis."

Maggie half expected him to swing a pocket watch in front of her eyes, but he merely made her lay back on the couch with her eyes closed and spoke softly next to her ear. She felt comfortable, safe and at peace. The pillows were soft and his reassuring voice was soporific. Maggie found herself dreaming, and yet still able to answer Dr Kressler's questions. She found herself voluntarily regressing to childhood; how lovely it was to see Tommy, her childhood cat, and Rocky her rabbit. She was running freely in the field behind her childhood home without a care in the world. She was quite sorry when Dr Kressler asked her to wake up.

"You are wonderful regression material." he told her. "I didn't ask you to regress - you were able to do that naturally. It is something I have used a lot in Germany, but we don't use regression much in the UK. Book in next week; we have a good canvass to work with."

Thus it was that Wednesday's saw Maggie taking the train for the forty or so miles to London to Wimpole Street. Wednesday was the quietest day in the shop and Anne felt she could easily manage the mornings without her.

On her third visit, Maggie found herself becoming Margaret de Pomerai.

"Where are you?" asked Dr Kressler.

Maggie told him she was in a lofty castle, lavishly furnished. Her language was difficult to understand as it was a mixture of early French and English. She told him the year was 1430 and her Lover Roger De Bouverie had taken her to his baronial home in Devon. He wanted to marry her and she was quite excited at the thought. Her parents disapproved of the match since the De Bouveries were not financially sound. They felt that he wanted her hand more for the dowry. This, they felt, might save his land and property from the creditors. There had been rumours of another lover, Maud Broase, but Roger soothed her fears. He made her feel special. She couldn't wait for the wedding. Dr Kressler woke her.

Feeling amazingly refreshed as usual, she had only a vague memory of her regression, more a fleeting feeling, like trying to remember a dream two hours after waking. Dr Kressler had made copious notes and discussed them with her. She could hardly wait for the next week.

Maggie almost didn't make the next appointment, however. The previous night she had cooked Roger a steak. He had demanded that it be blue; but Maggie, not being a lover of rare cooked meat, had served medium rare. The plate had cut her slightly, just above the eyebrow, as Roger threw it at her head. After he stormed out she had spent the evening cleaning up the wall and the carpet then sobbed herself to sleep. Naturally she overslept and only just managed to catch the train as the doors were closing.

She had soon relaxed on Dr Kressler's couch and almost immediately was back as Margaret - but she was now married and called Margaret De Bouverie. The wedding had been a quiet affair and Roger whisked her away to his home in Devon. He entertained lavishly but she was only allowed to watch from the gallery; she was not encouraged to join him when they had visitors. He had changed completely after the wedding. Their wedding night had been a trial for Margaret. Roger had shown no tenderness and after a quick and rather rough consummation had left her room. She heard him call for his horse and shout to his man that he would be spending the rest of the night at the home of Mistress Broase. Margaret cried herself to sleep and was so distressed that Dr Kressler became concerned for Maggie and woke her at once.

Under hypnosis, at the next visit, things had become worse. Roger had become a Hellraising drunkard. His gambling and debaucheries had become untenable. In one of his drunken rages, having lost at piquet, he offered her sexual favours as a means of paying his debt. This was a step too far, even for his drunken cronies, and a fight soon ensued. In his cups Roger stabbed one of his closest friends through the heart. In a fit of drunken remorse, he blamed Margaret and grabbing the shocked screaming woman he dragged her through the castle himself.

"You are useless!" He screamed "Not even good for the bedroom, No one else wants you and now you have made me kill a close friend, the finest knight I ever knew. You will pay for this!"

He ordered his manservant to open the unused dungeon. Dragging her by the hair, he took her to the smallest, darkest room. It had no window and measured about five feet by eight. He flung her into it and ordered the gaoler to seal the door with lime and horsehair.

"Rot there you useless, worthless witch!" And, with that, he was gone.

Maggie's screams alarmed Dr Kressler so much that he tried to bring her round but he could not wake her.

Margaret had calmed. Time had passed, she did not know how long, but hours and hours. Her hysteria had turned into low sobs. The room was black as pitch, not even the tiniest chink of light could penetrate the thick stone walls. Surely Roger didn't really mean to subject her to the oubliette? She would die of dehydration or suffocation before she would starve. She had no way of knowing how long she had been there. She was growing weak. The heat was oppressive and she felt so thirsty that the dehydration was making her delirious. Her dreams were jumbled, some, of her unhappy time with Roger, others of her dear childhood home, her loving parents. These were interspersed with odd moments of lucidity, when she despaired of her predicament. As she grew weaker though, the dreams took over and slowly the air turned foul.

In the cloying oppressive blackness Margaret saw a pin prick of light, down a long, long narrow tunnel. She thought she must be dreaming again since the room was tiny and the light was so distant. She crawled towards it. Her weakness and the struggle of movement sapped her strength; but slowly - so slowly - the light grew closer. Margaret felt herself being pulled towards the light. There was a rushing sound and then, suddenly, the light was so bright that she screwed up her eyes against it. She could hear cries - the cries of a baby - her cries. She opened her eyes to see the blurred image of a loving face; Maggie's Mother's face. Being born... Maggie woke up!

Dr Kressler's concerned face loomed over her.

"You had me worried. I couldn't wake you and you were so frightened." He began, but Maggie smiled, and cut him short:

"I know why I have developed my fear and I am over it now." She exclaimed triumphantly. "Death holds no fear for me anymore, it is just a rebirth to a new life".

She then told Dr Kressler all about Roger - both Rogers.

"I am striking out on my own now." She told him "No more abuse from him. I am stronger than that and will no longer tolerate it."

"One thing I still don't understand" She continued, "is why I leapt straight from the fifteenth century to the twentieth? To the day of my birth, even!"

Dr Kressler told her that chronological time is manmade "Who is to say that time may not run concurrently; that one day time travel may become a reality. Maybe we can cross dimensions; take that quantum leap - The grandfather paradox of modern physics...but that is for the physicists! For now I am just so glad I have been able to help you and you have taught me much too, young lady."

Anne persuaded her to move into the flat above the shop. The alarm system went straight through to the police station. This notified the police if anyone should attempt an unwelcome entry, so Maggie would be safe there. They went to her flat together to get Maggie's belongings. Like all bullies, Roger was a coward when faced with the wrath of two women, especially Anne, who told him that the police had been informed of his behaviour and he was never to come near Maggie again.

Once in the flat Anne helped Maggie to unpack.

"Do you want me to put your linen in the airing cupboard?" asked Anne.

"No thanks!" replied Maggie, "I am in control now. I can get myself out of the cupboard again! I can get myself out of any situation now. I am in control of my own destiny."

And she put the kettle on for coffee, (with no sugar!)

Kings Daughter

I loved this village and its dear little church. Dating back to Saxon times, it had retained many of its original features, mixed in with Norman alterations and Victorian pews. There was a strong sense of timelessness and all sound from the outside world ceased as the heavy wooden door closed.

Whenever I felt the need for spiritual enlightenment I would come here to this strange village by the sea with its ancient tidal harbour spreading up almost to the shops when the tide was in, its old Mill and the little church. My tour usually took in a walk by the harbour, a visit to the craft shops in the covered market, tea in the little café followed by some quiet contemplation in the church which, thankfully, was always unlocked.

It was a tiny building; a very small vestry at the back, then, down a few stone steps, a dark chapel which had once been the charnel house. This was the most atmospheric part of the church and made me aware of my own human frailty and how brief our lives are in the scheme of things. How much history had this church known?

Today I was in great need of spiritual uplifting. Soon it would be my only granddaughter's eighth birthday. Sadly I had only been able to speak to her through Skype early this morning as she and her parents, my daughter and son-in-law, had moved to America just four months previously. I missed them all dreadfully. I sat quietly in the church watching the dust dance in the weak rays of sunshine struggling through the tiny windows. Tears were filling my eyes and I looked up to stop them falling when I caught sight of something in the corner of my eye.

The impression I got was of a young girl, about seven or eight, standing by the lectern. She appeared to be wearing some sort of grey blanket with moccasins on her feet and straggly brown hair, braided like an American Indian girl. When I turned my head to look there was no one there.

I pulled myself together; the light was beginning to fail. It had been an emotional day for me (and a long one, being up so early to talk to Edith on Skype.) Time to go I thought.

On the way out of the church I placed an offering of coins in the wall safe and picked up a guide to the church which I put in my bag. "I must be missing Edith and my daughter so much that I imagined her in the church with me." I thought to myself. "The Indian style clothes are my subconscious acknowledgement that she is now in America" I went home to dinner and an early night.

On my next day off I returned to the village. It was only a few miles from my home town and I needed the bookshop and the craft centre. I wanted something to send to Edith for her birthday. It must be small enough to send through the post to America. The craft centre had lots of things to interest an eight year old girl. I spent quite a while looking around all of the shops, then chose a simple craft set of coloured beads with instructions to make a necklace and bracelet set - aged seven to nine years old - and flat enough to send airmail. The beads were amazingly pretty and, I thought, just right for Edith; she liked making things.

Today I walked down by the millstream. It was bright but quite chilly and the air felt winterish. It was very quiet and quite lonely by the stream. The water, although a trickle now, looked cold and uninviting. Just to my right, again in the corner of my eye, the same young girl appeared in her embroidered blanket dress and beads. Beads? I turned sharply but, once again, she was gone.

I headed to the church. I was earlier than usual, but I needed to sit down and it was a little too early for tea. It was very peaceful and quiet in the church, the thin wintry sun made a brave effort to shine through as I took out the bead kit and read the instructions. The colours were bright, varied and very attractive to an eight year old girl I thought. Suddenly she was there - solid as a real child. She stood to my right, just between the lectern and the chancel steps. The embroidered blanket dress was early English - very early - Saxon style, and the moccasins were calf skin shoes bound to the knee with leather. A plain child with reddish brown hair to her shoulders, freckles and grey eyes. She wore row upon row of coloured beads round her neck and forehead and braided in her hair. They were very similar to the ones I held in my hand. She smiled at me. Panic suddenly seized me! I grabbed my bag and flew out of the church into the weak sunshine and the comfort of the tea rooms. I had stopped shaking by my second cup of tea. To my horror

I found that I had left Edith's present in the church. I must go and retrieve it after tea.

I discovered the church guide still in my bag, unread from my visit the previous week. To steady my nerves I began to read it. On page three it mentioned, in passing, that a minor daughter of King Canute (by one of his concubines) had drowned whilst playing by the millstream. She was aged around eight years. It was thought that she was buried somewhere in the church, site unknown. "I know where now!" I thought. All at once I was seized with sympathy for this little, unimportant, forgotten child from long ago. On my way back to the church I picked a small posy of snowdrops from the path by the millstream.

The church was quiet and empty. Lying on the ground between the lectern and the chancel steps was the bead set, unopened and unharmed. Picking it up I replaced it with the snowdrops. "You will not be forgotten, darling." I said as I left the empty church.

Ari's Game

Keep your head down and stay out of sight, that's what they had told me before I took this journey. I hadn't the means to get anywhere unless I stowed away. That is exactly what I had done - slipping in the very back of the container lorry just before the driver drove onto the ferry, with no idea how I was going to get off unnoticed or where I would go when we arrived on that new, strange shore.

Somehow, luck was with me and I managed to stay undetected throughout the voyage and when we disembarked from the boat. I was weary and faint with hunger. When we stopped at a filling station for fuel, I slipped out by crawling underneath and dropping down in the early morning mist. Cutting across the road I headed for the cover of a small park on the opposite side, where I rested for a couple of hours until lunchtime. On the other side of the park was a residential road where I quickly found a large house with some windows open in the early summer heat.

I quietly crawled along, under the drawing room window sill, so as to be out of the view of the occupants of the room. I really needed to get in through the kitchen window at the back of the house, which I hoped they had left open. I didn't mean to take much; just a little sustenance to keep body and soul together, then I would be on my way - they need never know I had been here. I was starving, and desperate. This was how I was forced to live, a fugitive constantly on the run, prey to so many and a social outcast.

I forced a silent entry through the window and took a long, much needed, drink. I managed a quick bite of something they had left out and wouldn't miss, and then I effected an undetected escape – well almost! I had failed to see the young girl playing on the lawn with her little terrier dog. I dropped down from the open window onto the flower bed just as she came to fetch her ball and, of course, she spotted me. Boy! Could she scream loudly for one so small! I legged it as fast as I could but Fido, the terrier, had spotted me and gave chase, barking and yapping furiously. I just made it up and over the garden wall my legs millimetres away from his snapping jaws!

"Phew!" I thought, "I'm getting too old for this lark!"

I had nowhere to go, nobody wanted me around. Everywhere I went was fine at first, but, once I was found out, it became too dangerous for me to stay; as for women - huh! I had finished with them for good! Too treacherous; they were poison! They squeezed the life out of you, devouring your heart and soul; never satisfied, No, I was better off alone -travelling light, with no baggage.

I headed for the small park again and hid in the bushes to rest awhile and get my breath back. I had just decided that yonder bench would make a good bed for the night, when a courting couple lay down behind my hedge. This was rather embarrassing as they were oblivious to my presence - being full of desperate passion and desire for each other! I didn't quite know where to look, entertaining as this was, I knew that me being there was very wrong! I should try to creep away silently. I almost got away with it, too, but, at the last minute, the girl spotted me.

"Aaaaarrrrrgh! Arrgh! Arrgh!" she screamed.

"Oh, Baby!" said the guy.

"No you idiot!" She screamed, "Look!" - pointing at my retreating rear end.

He leapt up, looking really mad, and would have given chase but for his jeans (which had fallen around his ankles.) As I ran away again I thought how tiresome this was becoming. I didn't mean to keep scaring people, but this country was becoming impossible to hide in. The sky immediately overhead became momentarily darker.

I really needed to shelter quickly somewhere I would not be spotted. Things were getting desperate. I dived into the nearest shop doorway; at least I would be safe here until first light. It was most uncomfortable, but would do for now. Tomorrow I really must find a more permanent, safe, haven. Just as I was settling down for an uncomfortable night a small brown dog on a lead pulled into the doorway. He had the nerve to cock his leg on me! I didn't dare to move in case I drew attention to myself, as the dog's owner hadn't seen me. He hauled him off into the dark while I spent a cold damp night, shivering. Tomorrow I really must get out of the town!

At the first spark of dawn, a small delivery van pulled up outside the shop. The driver got out and walked round to the side of the van on the opposite side to me. I quickly crept out of the doorway and hid in front of the van. As he came out from the back with some crates of milk in his arms, I slunk into the back and hid. He slammed the rear doors without a glance inside and I was on the road again. Out into the countryside, I had heard, there was a special safe place for the likes of me. Somewhere I could hide from the world, and yet still survive well.

After some miles the van stopped at a roadside café to deliver some more milk. I hid behind the back crates until he had gone into the café, then I jumped out and ran off down the open country road. I kept to the hedgerows, with head down, so as to be as inconspicuous as possible - diving behind the hedges at the approach of every car. After what seemed like miles I saw the place I was looking for. It was up ahead on the right. Weak, hungry and rather exhausted, I staggered into this safe place. There was plenty of good food, and I was, I discovered, absolutely famished.

“Oh look!“ said a voice. It belonged to a pretty young female volunteer. “A beautiful harvest spider! Hello, and welcome to the South Downs Nature Reserve, Mr Arachnid!”

“Actually,” I said with my mouth full (as I heartily devoured a freshly trapped fly), “I’m an exotic spider and my name is Ari! Ari Ackney.“

But I don’t think she heard me.

The Secret of the Old Grammar School

"Tock, are you awake?" whispered Jimmy 'Tadpole' Frogley.

George McClochry opened one eye.

"What's up, Tadpole" he asked groggily.

"Listen!" said the other boy, "There it is again."

Tock strained his ears. He fancied he could just hear a faint, low moan, but he couldn't be sure.

"Probably the wind; go back to sleep." He muttered.

But Tadpole Frogley was having none of it. "Only wind I can hear is Roly Rowlands after all that curry at supper! No, Tock, listen! I can hear her sobbing."

This had been going on for the last few nights, about half an hour after lights out – strange, faint noises could be heard by the two boys, apparently coming from the attic above their dormitory.

Tock and Tadpole were 13 year old boarders; pupils at the old Grammar School in Rye. The building was centuries old and had its own strange creaks and groans - more noticeable in the quietness of the night. As they were debating the source of the noise, a louder, unmistakable, thump came from directly above their heads. Only the empty attic lay above the boy's top dormitory. The boys looked at each other for a second or two

"Come on." said Tadpole, "We need to settle this once and for all."

They slipped out of bed not even stopping to pull dressing gowns over their striped pyjamas or slide their freezing feet into slippers.

"All clear" announced Tock, in a barely audible whisper.

He had peeped out of the door to check the corridor was empty, and then they crept silently out of the dormitory and ran to the back stair door. Slipping through it they crept up the old staircase, their nervousness increasing with every creaky stair. The door to the attic room was locked and bolted, with padlocks on each bolt, top and bottom. A large sign on the door proclaimed "Keep Out" in bold capitals. All was quiet, the boys strained their ears but no sound could be heard anywhere.

"Let's go back to bed, it's freezing and my feet are congealing on the lino!" whispered Tock.

But as the words left his mouth a sound like a footstep came from behind the door. The boys froze, terror beginning to grip them, then a sigh was heard, a heart rending sigh, epitomising hopeless sorrow and grief. Tadpole's blood froze in his veins and he would have turned tail and run, but Tock was on his knees looking through the keyhole in the attic door.

"What is it? What can you see?" hissed Tadpole.

Tock could see nothing but blackness at first, and then, as his eyes adjusted, he saw a moonbeam across the floor from the dormer window in the attic roof. He was just about to proclaim the room empty when he saw a shadow cross the moonbeam; an unusually tall, thin shadow, he fancied he saw a thin white ankle in a ladies black slipper. Just as he saw this the sound of a soft footfall could be heard.

"Here Tadpole, look!" He turned to his friend to be faced with Mr Willis, the housemaster. He was holding Tadpole by the ear and was not looking very happy.

"What is this?" He growled, in a dour voice.

The boys assumed this was a rhetorical question!

"Sorry Mr Willis, sir, we thought we heard a noise, sir." blustered the boys.

"In which case you come and get me, you don't wander around out of bounds sticking your grubby little noses where they shouldn't be! Come and see me after lessons tomorrow, three strokes each!"

The cane! The boys expected nothing less, luckily only three. It could have been half a dozen! They went back to the dorm, but, just as Tadpole was dozing off, Tock hissed at him to look out of the window. Hurrying across the green towards the main gate was a stocky little man with a military bearing and an old fashioned moustache. He was furtively scurrying along and appeared to be wearing clothes from some twenty years earlier. Neither boy recognised him, but they guessed he must be a visitor; maybe on his way to a fancy dress ball and straying into the school grounds by mistake.

The following afternoon, after lessons, the boys went to face their punishment. Their way back to the house necessitated a walk around the back of the building. It was 4.30 on a cold winter's afternoon. Already it was dusk. Glancing up in the gloom Tadpole caught his breath and grabbed Tock's arm. He pointed up at the attic dormer. Usually in darkness, it was now eerily glowing with a flickering candlelight, peering from the window was a female face. A pale emaciated face with straggly black hair framing it and falling onto her shoulders. Her eyes seemed like black holes against the pallor of her complexion. The boys ran into the building and bumped straight into Mr Willis. Both trying to apprise him of the vision in the window, they gabbled incoherently until he seized them each by the shoulder. Their shocked faces softened him somewhat.

"Come into my study and tell me what you have discovered." he said.

He listened patiently to their story.

"I don't disbelieve you, but you must keep this to yourselves. If you see or hear anything suspicious again, don't alarm the other boys, come and get me."

The following Saturday afternoon was a free period for the boys when they were allowed out for a couple of hours. They usually went into the town to buy comics and sweets unavailable in the school tuck shop. Rye was very busy as was usual for Saturdays, with people frantically shopping. There were horses and carriages vying for space in the narrow cobbled streets and the odd motor car blocking the road - the chauffeurs bandying words with the coachmen, while their employers ordered laces and other trinkets in the shops.

That night the noises in the Attic were so plentiful and piteous that the boys woke Mr Willis. They listened. A heart-rending sobbing was heard with pacing footsteps. When they went up to the attic door and shone Mr Willis' lantern through the keyhole nothing could be seen and the noises stopped abruptly. Mr Willis told them to go back to bed and leave it to him. They obeyed reluctantly but noticed that he looked thoughtful. Monday afternoon, straight after school, he disappeared and did not return until nearly six-o-clock, just before supper.

"Come and see me in my study after you've eaten." he told the boys.

Mr Willis had visited the local newspaper offices and had been reading through back issues of some twenty years previously.

"I had heard the legend," he began, "but didn't believe it until you heard those noises, so I went to play detective and found out more than I expected."

He told them the following tale:

At the turn of the twentieth century a Headmaster, Major Blanding, was living at the school with his wife, Theodora. A short, stocky, man, he sported a magnificent waxed moustache – fashionable at the time. She was a tall woman, of a very nervous disposition and prone to bouts of melancholia and ill temper. She would lock herself in her room for hours on end when the humour was upon her and would refuse all sustenance. This unhappy union drove Major Blanding to strike up a friendship with a Mrs Adelaide Frobisher - a young widow in the town who lived in a fine town house in Market Street. This was not far from the school. It appears that they fell very much in love, but the stumbling block to their happiness was the, then, current Mrs Blanding. She disappeared one day and was never seen again. The story was given out by the Major that she had run off in a fit of temper and deserted him. He and Mrs Frobisher waited a decent period then left the town together. Rumour had it that they married as soon as his marriage to Theodora was officially declared over.

This would have been the end of it, but stories were whispered in the school that Major Blanding had locked his wife in the attic whilst he visited his lover; leaving Theodora to starve. Some of the boys had seen her emaciated face peering out of the attic dormer in the days before she disappeared. The Major had dismissed this as 'her ladyship' locking herself in, in a fit of pique.

Some ten years after Major Blanding and Mrs Frobisher left the town, some workmen, fixing a water tank in the attic, found the emaciated body of Theodora under the floorboards. She had, apparently, starved to death. Of her murderous husband and his paramour no trace could be found!

"But why is it all still locked up?" asked Tadpole.

"Yes, and why can we still hear her?" questioned Tock.

"Let's find out!" exclaimed Mr Willis.

He had borrowed some strong bolt-cutters from the school handyman. Lighting a lantern, he and the boys headed up the staircase to the attic door. Tock held the lantern while Mr Willis cut the padlocks. Tadpole was secretly afraid and held back behind the others. Finally the last lock was cut through, the bolt drawn back and the door swung open. A strange musty smell filled their nostrils and a frantic whirring filled the air. Tadpole fell to his knees, his arms over his head.

"Wait!" cried Tock, "Bats! It's only bats - hundreds of them!"

Sure enough the room was full of nesting bats hanging upside down from the rafters or flying crazily back and forth as the light disturbed them. Some of them were screeching and their wings made a whirring noise like a sigh.

"There's your noises in the night, boys!" said Mr Willis. "The attic is a breeding ground for bats. Let's close the door and leave them to their own devices."

They agreed and went back to their dormitory, but, as they settled for the night, the boys felt that the attic would never again know peace!

All Over By Christmas

Sarah was thrilled, another baby at last. She and Thomas Shore, her husband had given up hope of a brother or sister for Katie, and now the doctor had told her to expect a new arrival about February time. Three months gone! No wonder she had felt so tired and sickly. Problem was that February was the beginning of the lambing season, the busiest time here at Fairfield Farm. Still she told herself, with dad here to help and young Albert from the village, they should manage. Katie could help a little too. She was eight years old and could help in the kitchen. She would tell Thomas the good news when he got in from town. He needed something to cheer him up. He had been very stirred up that morning about Britain becoming involved in the crisis on the continent. This was August 1914 and Britain had just declared war on Germany. Thomas came home just in time for dinner and, as they sat at table, Sarah prepared to tell him the good news. He spoke first:

"Now don't be angry, my dear!" He said, "Captain Blackmore was drumming up support for a local regiment to join the latest fight. I have joined up and I leave next week for France."

Seeing her face, he added "Don't worry, darling, it will all be over by Christmas. We will give the Kaiser a real drubbing."

His eyes were bright with excitement and he was so animated that she didn't have the heart to worry him with her news. If he knew her condition, he would doubtless stay home. She knew how much he valued his principles and that was why she smiled encouragement and held her tongue.

The following week Sarah went with Thomas to the station to wave him off. How handsome the men all looked in their uniforms thought Sarah; full of courage and righteousness; marching off to teach Kaiser Bill a lesson. She admired Thomas for having the strength of his convictions, but, nonetheless, she had a huge lump in her throat as she waved her handkerchief until the train was out of sight. If things really were all over by Christmas, then there would be time enough for Thomas to get used to the idea of becoming a father again. Meanwhile, she would get her bottom drawer together with the layette for the new arrival and she, dad and poor young Albert would keep the farm ticking over until lambing, by which time Thomas should be home. Fairfield was one of the largest sheep farms on Walland Marsh and Sarah knew that both Thomas and his father would love a boy to carry on the Shore family farm. Soon she would have to tell dad, but she would swear him to secrecy as far as Thomas was concerned. She wanted the pleasure of telling him herself once he was safely home.

September passed, then October brought the first tingles of winter chill with it. The nights had drawn in, the fire was alight day and night and Sarah lit fires in the bedrooms for the first time that season. Luckily this was a fairly quiet time on the farm. Sarah's pregnancy was beginning to show a little now. She loosened her apron and wore it a little lower, but soon she would have to tell people. Then, one day in late October, she walked into the village. In the village shop she heard the dreadful news. There had been a mighty battle on the Somme. Some of the local lads had been killed and many more missing, presumed dead. For the first time, the vague nagging unease that Sarah had felt for Thomas became a fear and a sick worry. She had received a few letters from him in which he told her that his farming experience had stood him in good stead to look after the horses that pulled the gun carriages. He loved the horses and it reminded him of how much he missed Sampson, the farm's Clydesdale; how very much he missed them all. In his last letter Sarah had the feeling that he was holding something back from her. He had not sounded his usual positive self and had been rather vague about the conditions he and his comrades were living in. Weeks flew by, although the sickness in the mornings had passed, Sarah could no longer hide her swollen belly. She told dad, but swore him to secrecy. There were other worries. The most serious one was that she had received no letter from Thomas since late October. It was now late November!

"No news is good news "Dad told her, trying to ease her mind.

But she could tell he was as worried as she was. Why hadn't she heard from him? From what she had been told, this war was very unlikely to be over by Christmas, it would be fortunate if it were over by Christmas 1915! Was this baby to be born without a father? She needed Thomas, where was he? Sarah found herself lying awake at night thinking about him. Every morning she ran to meet the postman, only to be disappointed and relieved at the same time. Disappointed that there was no letter from Thomas, and relieved that there was no black-edged envelope from the War Office.

The plum pudding was maturing in the cold larder. The cake mix had been well laced with brandy and Sarah was busying herself making mince pies to take her mind off her troubles. There was still no news of Thomas. She tried to keep faith that he would return as he had promised and spent a day shopping for Christmas presents. She bought some slippers and a new pipe for dad, the dolls pram that Katie had been asking for (complete with a dolly). As a sign of that faith she went a step further than usual and bought a fine pair of silver cufflinks for Thomas as if, by buying them, it would ensure his safe homecoming.

Finally Christmas Eve arrived. A freezing cold crisp day it was too. The morning was spent with Katie in the woods collecting holly and ivy to decorate the house. As a special treat she had allowed Katie a small tree inside the house this year, Dad had cut them a fine spruce of about 4 feet in height. She and Katie had been busy making paperchains and baking glazed dough in the shape of stars. These, with dried orange slices, would be hung by threads from the branches by way of decoration. Katie was especially proud of a large paper star which Sarah had painted and hung from the top of the tree. Earlier that day they had helped the ladies of the village decorate the church for the Christmas services. A much larger tree than theirs stood to the right of the altar and the pleasant smell of pine filled the tiny medieval building. Sarah would go to the service on Christmas morning as she didn't like leaving Katie and dad alone in the house for too long in the evenings. She had prepared a fine goose for the Christmas feast. Now they sat by the fire wrapped in shawls in an attempt to keep warm. They finished a paperchain garland. Sarah went over the preparations in her mind to ensure that nothing was forgotten for the big day on the morrow. She was determined to make it as pleasant as possible for dad and Katie's sake, but she felt wretched. For the first time she despaired; her first Christmas without Thomas.

"He's not coming home for Christmas." She thought. "He's never coming home again! This baby will not know its father!"

It was as much as she could do to hide her despair from Katie and dad. The girl was tiresome at bedtime and didn't want to sleep - natural enough with the excitement of Christmas - but Sarah found it difficult to cope with this year. Sarah read to her until finally she fell asleep. She then, quickly and quietly, filled her stocking with an orange, some crayons and a small sketchbook and, as a special treat, some sugared almonds. She and dad had a final cocoa together by the fire before going off to their beds.

Sarah found she couldn't sleep. Her pregnancy had got to the uncomfortable stage and whichever way she lay was burdensome to her. She was shivering in the big bed all alone despite her hot water bottle and the fire in the room. She just couldn't stop the thoughts in her head. She worried about the baby not knowing a father and about how she would manage the lambing season with a new born baby and just dad and Albert. Dads heart was not up to it, supposing something happened to him too. How would she manage? When she did finally manage to sleep, she kept having jumbled and disturbing dreams about Thomas; he was lying injured in some French field, or worse. Finally, about 5am, she was obliged to get up and visit the outside privy. It was a freezing cold but beautifully clear morning. There was a bright full moon and the sky was full of bright stars. The frost crunched under her feet as she pulled her shawl closer around her shoulders. Getting back into the house, she coaxed the fires back to life and put a match under the kettle for morning tea.

"No point in going back to bed now!" She thought.

She suddenly remembered that it was Christmas morning. The clock ticked a soporific tick-tock. The kettle hissed gently. She had a sudden impulse to slip across the field to the little village church to say a prayer for Thomas. Was he alive? If so was he looking at those same stars just a few miles across the sea? She quietly ran upstairs and slipped into her clothes. Pulling on her boots and fastening her shawl into her belt she stopped briefly to listen outside Katie's door, no sound except gentle snoring. Sarah grabbed her lantern, lit it and she slipped out of the back door. She hurried across the crisp frosty grass to the church.

The little church looked beautiful in the lantern light. Sarah lit some of the candles at the end of the pews left from last night's midnight service. She knelt on a hassock in the front pew and clasping her hands together, closed her eyes and tried to pray. The tears then flowed freely. She started softly weeping but weeks of anguish finally gave way and she burst into the most violent, raking sobs. She was sobbing so loudly that she failed to hear the gentle click of the door latch at the back of the church. When her sobs subsided she heard her name softly called. At first she thought she had imagined it, she stood and turned to look over her shoulder. He stood in the shadows at the back of the church half hidden.

She never knew which of them was the most surprised - Thomas at seeing her swollen belly or her at his crutches and empty left trouser leg pinned up below the knee! There was much hugging and tears on both sides. Sitting on the front pew in the little medieval candlelit church he told her of the first Battle of the Somme and how he and his battalion had just gone 'Over the top' when a massive shell exploded! Waking up in a military hospital he realised his war was over. His left leg was gone from the knee down. He wrote her a letter himself to explain since he didn't want an official letter to arrive and worry them all. He was horrified to hear that she had never received it. Not hearing back from her had troubled him so he had insisted on early repatriation and arrived in Dover very late on Christmas Eve. He just managed to catch the milk train to Appledore and got a lift to Brookland with the dairy carter who was on his way home for Christmas. He limped the last few miles across the marsh. Passing the Church on his way to the farm he saw it lit up and popped in to give a prayer of thanks! He seemed very shocked at Sarah's condition but delighted too.

"You should have told me." He said. "I could have been killed and died not knowing that I was a father again."

Sarah felt justifiably chastened. With a sigh of relief she stood and put her arm around his waist as they headed to the church door.

"I thank God that you weren't killed!" She murmured.

She knew now that Thomas was home they could cope somehow with the lambing season, they could cope with anything!

"Come on!" she said, decisively. "Breakfast, we'll be back for the morning service soon, as a whole family!"

"I don't have a gift for you" said Thomas.

"Your homecoming is the best gift anyone could ever have!" she told him.

They opened the church door onto a greyish dawn light outside was a white winter wonderland. Huge soft flakes of snow were falling, looking black against the early dawn sky.

"It's snowing! Perfect. Merry Christmas, darling." exclaimed Thomas.

Sarah knew that now it really would be a Merry Christmas.

The Dark Lantern

Maria put her head down and pedalled faster. It was dark now, the rain had turned to icy sleet and she only had a very dim light on her bicycle. Why, oh why, hadn't she listened to her husband, Phil, and taken the car. She had insisted that her bike would be quicker - "Easier to hop on and off and no parking problems." she had told him.

As the new secretary of the local WI, she had been keen to show willing and deliver personally the parish magazines to the housebound and elderly members of the community. She was new to the area having moved down from Brighton, so was unfamiliar with the place. This small Romney Marsh village and surrounding areas should only take a couple of hours at most she thought to herself. She hadn't bargained on some of the lonely folk she visited wanting a cosy chat or insisting that she have a warming cuppa with them. Now it was dark and the falling temperature was causing the roads to glisten with frost, the rain had turned to sleet. Too late she recalled Phil's warning of black Ice on the more rural, less used roads. She suddenly felt the handlebars wrenched out of her hands as the bike slewed sideways and then over, catapulting her into the ditch at the roadside. As her head struck the frozen ground, she felt an explosion of stars behind her eyes before blackness and unconsciousness overtook her. She came to almost immediately and cursed her haste in leaving home as she had left her bag, complete with mobile phone on the hall table. This was a quiet country lane, little used by traffic either foot or motorised. No public 'phone boxes here and precious few dwellings as far as she could recall. Apart from a dull headache and a twisted ankle and elbow, she thought she was alright, so she turned left to the direction she had been travelling in and limped off on foot to find civilization.

After about a quarter of a mile, she spotted a small row of cottages on the right of the lane the end two were in total darkness but the middle one had a very dim flickering light showing through the red checked curtains, summoning up her courage and hoping she didn't look too dishevelled in the stormy conditions she limped up the path and lifted the heavy iron door knocker. Within a few seconds the door was opened by a little bent old man in moleskin trousers with a black jacket, shiny with age, he looked enquiringly at her.

"I'm terribly sorry to trouble you," she launched at once into her predicament, "I have just skidded my bicycle on some dratted black ice and I seem to have hurt myself a little. I wonder, could I use your 'phone to contact my husband, he can come and collect me.." she broke off as the little man cut across her.

"Come in, come on in, Missy, 'tis freezing with the door open. You have no business to be out on bicycles in weather like this and in the dark too – ain't safe I tell 'ee Come in by the fire."

Entering straight into a small living room Maria noticed that the dim flickering light had been caused by candles and an ancient gas lamp.

“Oh poor old thing, a powercut.“ She thought, “Hardly surprising in this bad weather though.”

She was secretly very grateful for the sit down. Her head ached fearfully and she was bone cold with wet clothes where she had fallen into the grassy ditch. The cottage, though dim, was surprisingly warm and cosy. There were just two dark buckskin armchairs each side of the little iron fireplace which contained a small but roaring fire, over the high wooden mantle was a picture mirror with rather faded paintings of sheep each side of the spotted aged mirror. The ormolu clock on the mantle ticked softly and a small table covered with a heavy chenille dull red cloth completed the sparse furnishings. What struck Maria the most though was the quietness and oppressive atmosphere. No sound at all came from outside and a feeling of pressure in her ears added to the strangeness of it all. She put it down to her blow to the head. The little man was pouring something into a glass and shuffling back towards her.

“Here, m’dear, drink this, it will warm you. You must keep warm. No night to be out on the marsh, you can freeze on a night like this in no time. Come closer to the fire.“

Maria thought her shins would roast if she moved any closer but she gratefully took the drink with an enquiring look.

“My best parsnip wine.“ said the man proudly. “A particularly good batch, even though I say it myself.”

"If I could use your 'phone?" persisted Maria.

"Ha!" chuckled the old man, "There ain't no telephone for miles round here, no post office near see, but I can give you a light. That's the ticket, a light. Can't let you out on a night like this without a good light so as folk can see you in the dark."

Maria began to think that the old man may be a bit simple, as if guessing her thoughts he etched a little bow and stuck out a thin wrinkled hand

"Jonas" he said, "Jonas Walls"

"Maria Prescott." said Maria, shaking his hand.

Jonas continued: "I had an accident on my bike once on just such a night, Only just out of autumn, yet freezing, icy roads already. I was coming down this lane on my way home from the farm, skidded on the ice and knocked meself out. Well, I 'ad no lights, see? Pitch black and fool Jonas with no lights and lying witless in the ditch, No one knew I was there. I was frozen!"

"Oh poor you." said Maria, "Were you there long?"

"All blessed night!" said Jonas, with a chuckle and a mirthful smile, "But not you Missy, Old Jonas will give ye a lanthorn to light ye home."

He disappeared into the next room and Maria finished her glass of strong, yet surprisingly good, wine. He came back with an ancient dark lantern, the sort the old lookers on the marsh used to use.

"Oh!" exclaimed Maria, "That is surely an antique. I couldn't possibly risk..."

But Jonas looked Hurt. "Now, Missy, please! I insist." He sounded so concerned that Maria felt obliged to take it.

"I will take great care of it and get my husband to return it to you tomorrow. Now I should be going – thank you so much for the warm up and the excellent wine."

Jonas looked earnestly into her eyes; "Please, Missy, take care!" he said. "Use the lanthorn and wrap up really warm."

He stooped and, taking her outstretched hand, he gave the back of it a little brush with his lips while etching that funny bow. As the cottage door closed behind her, the oppressive feeling overtook Maria and she felt a little lonely and afraid as she hurried up the lane towards her damaged bike. As she approached she saw a small knot of people peering into the ditch and two cars parked on the grass verge. One of them was Phil's but hardly had this registered than she felt the whole world swim in a blurry circle before her eyes, she stumbled and felt herself falling. When she awoke it was to see faces looking down at her. The most worried face of all was Phil.

"She's coming round!" he said. "Where is that Ambulance?"

Maria realised that she was back in the ditch, frozen and wet. I must have dreamed the cottage she thought, but, in her hand she held the dark lantern.

She had never thought of hospital beds as being particularly comfortable before, but the clean crisp sheets, warmth and dryness of being in one was sheer luxury after the cold wet ditch. Phil was fussing over her and kept peering into her eyes in a most concerned way. He was unpacking her clean clothes from a small overnight bag that he had brought from home. Maria had been kept in hospital overnight for observation. She had concussion, badly bruised ribs and a sprained ankle, Comfortable was how they had described her condition to Phil.

"Huh", she thought "Not much comfort with these injuries!" But then, it could have been much worse, and would have been had Phil not come looking for her. She supposed she should be grateful for small mercies. After a fairly sleepless night, Phil was allowed to take her home as long as she rested for at least 48 hours. She limped out on his arm to the car with her ankle strapped up feeling very battle scarred, but grateful.

"Did you bring the old man's lantern?" she asked Phil, "We can return it on the way home."

"Do stop fussing!" Phil told her, "I have it here, but there is no hurry."

"But I want to get it back to him safely and thank him for looking after me last night. He was so worried about the dark, and, if he loses power in the cottage again, He may need it, the cottage is on the way home."

They turned into the lane where she had come a cropper and drove slowly past the ditch, how innocent the lane looked today in the light, just crisp and cold, no sleet, frost or ice today.

"It must be just up here on the right." said Maria.

After a quarter of a mile or so of nothing but fields a large barn built of corrugated iron and steel girders appeared, it was almost full of round hay bales.

"The cottages must be near here." said Maria, "I didn't walk this far!"

"Did you pass the barn?" queried Phil.

"I don't think so, but it was dark, so maybe I did." said Maria doubtfully.

"We've done nearly two miles, you couldn't have walked this far with your ankle." said Phil, "Are you sure it is on this road?"

They drove up and down the lane and then drove a five mile circuitous route; yet, no cottages at all could they find. There was just the odd big house reposing up long driveways. Maria felt close to tears

"That's IT!" said Phil assertively. "We are going home now, you are done in. This can wait."

Later, as he helped her to put her ankle up on a foot stool she said "Will you drive me to the garden centre tomorrow please? I want to see my friend, Sue. She knows every inch of this area and every family, every house. She will know where Jonas Walls lives."

Sue was a bubbly blonde lady with a ready smile who had spent all her life living on the marsh. She worked at a small garden centre which conveniently had a coffee shop. Having settled Maria into a seat in the coffee shop, and ensured Sue was able to take her coffee break at that time too, Phil left them with their frothy coffees and went off to the tropical fish section.

"I don't know a Jonas Wall but there have been Wall's living in this area for donkey's years." Sue told her, "There was a row of three cottages in that lane but they were destroyed by fire in the early '70's. Providence Cottages had been built around the 1850's or 60's I think. They were part of the big farm and built for the workers. As the farm got sold off piecemeal, the cottages were rented to short term tenants. In the early 1970's the owner was having them renovated when a builder's blowtorch caught the window frame alight in the middle one. The fire spread at an alarming pace to the others. The damage was so extensive that the owner had them demolished and the barn erected instead. You must have had a real bad blow to the head!"

Sue's pleasant face lit up with a grin and they finished their coffee break with more general chit chat.

Maria went straight to her laptop when she got home. A short search found her the Kent Coroners Court archives. After an hour's searching she found the report she had been looking for. Dated 1925 it read "Deceased, one Jonas Walls following a tragic fall from his bicycle in inclement weather on 31st October 1925. Head injury and bruising. Cause of death – Hypothermia.

She went on to read that Jonas had fallen from his bike into the ditch, just like her. His Bicycle had only had a dark dynamo light fitted, which soon flickered out. In the dark, and with very little passing horse or foot traffic, no-one could see him. He wasn't found until daybreak – he simply froze to death. Hot tears blurred her eyes and Phil found her sobbing into her hankie when he came in with her lunch. He placed the antique lantern in pride of place on their mantelpiece.

"Tomorrow," he told her, "we will go to the churchyard with some flowers, we'll find his resting place and you can thank him properly."

But Maria did not answer, she was lost in thought staring at the lantern; in a faraway place of her own!

Murder on the Marsh

"Shame about Eddie Whiterose, still quite young and those two young boys too – ugh, not cheese and pickle again!"

PC Graham Jessop was opening a greaseproof wrap of sandwiches as he imparted the latest local news to Will. Sergeant Will Simmons and Graham had been friends for several years and had been PCs together under Will's predecessor, old Sergeant Watson, before he retired. Will had wanted to get on and move up the ranks; while Graham was a faithful plodder who was very happy to stay a PC, but was, none the less, a good effective copper.

"Yes, poor chap! So sudden too." said Will, shuffling his paperwork and looking speculatively at his lunchpack on the desk. What had his new wife Sally given him today? He wondered.

He said, "Still, at least Beth and the boys have George and Rick to keep the farm going. No shortage of money there - they should be alright."

Whiterose farm was one of the biggest sheep and arable farms in the area, and one of the oldest too. It had been in the same family for generations and was situated on the old road to Midley. Eddie had been the eldest of the three Whiterose brothers, and, therefore, had inherited the farm on the death of their father. The modern farming methods of the 1950's meant that working the land was less labour intensive. The brothers could manage with just a couple of local workers and a few casual labourers to help at shearing and lambing time. This meant that, instead of staying in the big farmhouse as one big family like generations of Whiteroses had done before, Rick and George were able to move into two of the labourer's cottages on the estate when Eddie had married Beth. Rick had never married and was a bookish, quiet man. He showed no interest in the farm. He was the only brother to go to university and became a teacher at a small private school in the area. He loved literature, kept his own council and spent any free time reading. George was the opposite; a lazy, raucous, heavy drinking womaniser who made the life of his young wife, Bella, a misery. His job was to keep the farm accounts, but Eddie suspected that he falsified them on occasions. He was a byword in the local pubs, and any decent woman kept well away when he was on a binge. Beth and Eddie had been the only ones to produce children -two sons, Edward and Richard, currently away at school in Sussex; now their father, Eddie, had succumbed after a short, illness. He died of renal failure, which was thought to have been a complication of his diabetes.

"The funeral's next Wednesday." said Graham, " I expect the poor boys will be allowed home from school for the occasion; how tragic for them!"

"True," said Will "but at least the family should still be able to afford the school fees, and keep the farm going for the elder lad to inherit."

The routine of policing took up the next few days; then it was the funeral of Eddie Whiterose. Will and Graham paid their respects to the family after the service before returning to police duties. Will noticed that Beth was pale and seemed somewhat lost, but the two boys were stuck like limpets to their uncle Rick, who was somewhat over protective to them.

Life returned to normal at the police station and the weeks passed. Then, one morning Graham took a call:

"Sarg, its Whiterose Farm. Mr George has been found dead this morning – seems he drowned in the sheep dip channel!"

When Will and Graham arrived at the farm, Bella was dry-eyed and sullen. She answered only in words of one syllable, and seemed less grief stricken and more composed than poor Beth, who was pale and weepy, while being most solicitous to Bella. Rick was looking shocked and distant. He kept drumming his fingers on the kitchen table in the farmhouse. No they hadn't seen him at all this morning. Yes he had been drinking last night - had a skinfull by all accounts – and, according to Rick, had made much noise singing as he passed his cottage at about 11.30. No, Bella hadn't thought it odd that he didn't come to bed with her; they often slept in separate rooms, especially when he had been out on a bender! Dr Bray was in attendance as they went to the body. The Scene of Crime team were taking photographs. George was lying on his stomach with his arms stretched out over the top of the trough. He was face down in the liquid with most of his head submerged; only the back of his head was showing. Dr Bray gave permission for them to remove him from the trough.

"He's been dead for at least 5 hours, I'd say." He said. "Sometime between midnight and 5am at a guess - but I'll know more after the PM. Okay lads." He nodded permission for them to take the body to the undertakers van for removal to the mortuary.

Will thought, not for the first time, how tenuous and fragile life was. The last time he had seen George alive he'd been getting outside a bottle of scotch at Eddie's funeral. Now he was stiff, blue and silent forever. He must have had a real skinfull at the pub and fallen into the trough in the dark.

Walking back to the car with Graham they bumped into Beth running out of the house.

"Bella seems okay - Rick's with her. I must tell the boys." She gasped, clamping her hand to her mouth wide-eyed.

"How can I tell them? How will they take it so soon after their father?"

She broke off. Rick approached her, placing his hands on her shoulders.

He said "Leave them until tomorrow. Bring them home again for a few days. I'll look after them. They need a man's reassurance at this time. You all do."

He buried his nose in her hair and she leant her head back on his chest. Will left them standing like this deep in conversation as he drove back to the station.

The following morning Will took a call from Sussex Police. Edward and Richard Whiterose were missing from their school. Beth had arrived just after breakfast to break the news to the boys. They were nowhere to be found, and their friends could not remember seeing them at breakfast. The police had started a search, but Will's team were alerted in case they came home.

"Poor Beth." Said Graham to Will when he heard the news.

"She has enough on her plate. She must be desperate with worry; they say trouble comes in threes."

As he finished Dr Bray came into the station.

"I was passing on my way to the farm." He said.

"You'll get the formal report but, for the record, George Whiterose was murdered!"

He told them there was bruising to the back of his head and across his stomach where he had been held under the sheep dip following a blow which had felled him in the first place.

"He wouldn't have known it was coming; no sign of a struggle. Probably never knew who his assailant was."

"It could be one of half a dozen disgruntled husbands!" retorted Graham.

"He preferred other men's wives to poor Bella!"

Will was dismayed. This meant that, not only was there a murderer in the area, but now he had to get the CID involved. Why was life so complicated? He wondered.

Days passed. There was no sign of the two brothers, either in Kent, or Sussex. Beth was desperate and Rick seemed more solicitous than ever to her. Bella busied herself cooking meals that no one wanted, and awaited the release of George's body for burial. The CID and Will had questioned every known contact of George's, both male and female. All had solid alibis. The one with perhaps the most motive was Bella, but she lacked the strength to hold her husband down in the dip.

One day, a week or so after the boys' disappearance, the village awoke to the first early frost of the season. It was a freezing, crisp morning. Will was driving the Old Romney Road when he saw Rick's car on the roadside. The bonnet was up and steam was pouring out of the engine. He pulled over and Rick straightened.

"Damn fool I was!" he said," With all the drama and misery, I forgot to put in the anti-freeze! She's boiled over."

Will went to the boot of his car to fetch the emergency can of water he always kept handy.

"Sorry about your nephews. Any news yet?"

"No, I'm afraid not. Beth is taking it all very badly. She really needs me at the moment - what with George yet to be buried, and Bella moping about like a mad Ophelia!"

Handing the empty can to Will, he said

"Thank you Sergeant. First sign that winter is upon us – truly, now IS the winter of our discontent!"

The words stuck with Will as he drove away. He was not very versed in Shakespeare, but at the back of his mind was the name of a play.... That's it – Richard the third! Just like Rick Whiterose! He was the Third - both his father and grandfather had been Richards. As the first born they had inherited the family farm. But Edward was the firstborn! And if his son can be found another Edward will inherit! What a mystery! A cold sinking fear in the pit of Will's stomach made him stop the car. He turned towards Snave. His old history teacher's cottage was there. Time for some after-school lessons he told himself.

Mr Gardener, his old teacher, was pleased to see him.

"Come near the fire lad!" He said as he handed him a cup of steaming tea, and settled opposite Will by the roaring blaze.

"Now, what do you want to know?"

"Tell me about Richard the third, please." replied Will.

An hour later Will walked into the police station.

"Graham! We need an exhumation order on Eddie Whiterose and get CID to put a tail on Rick Whiterose - yes! I said Eddie!"

Later that night a small tent was erected over the grave. Beth was white and trembling, and Rick was indignant.

"This is pointless! Shouldn't you be looking for the boys instead of dragging out the misery for poor Beth?"

He led her back to the house with a withering backward glance as the coffin was raised. Will noticed, however, that, once the household had settled, Rick sloped off followed by a furtive CID officer.

Will crept into bed in the early hours hoping not to wake Sally, his wife of four months. His mind was buzzing and he was frozen. She snuggled into his back and draped a warm arm and leg over him. Despite himself, he fell into a heavy sleep.

His Bedside phone woke him at 6.30am (after four hour sleep!) Richard had led them to the boys! They were safe and well and on their way home.

The boys had been well cared for. Richard had spirited them away from school with the offer of an adventure and paid a private nanny from an agency (with excellent references) to give them a holiday by the sea in Clacton. He had sworn them to secrecy as part of the adventure and arranged to meet them if they would slip away from school on their way to breakfast. He had given the nanny a false name and paid her in cash, as he did the landlady of the boarding house where they lodged. He now languished in the cells while the boys had an emotional reunion with Beth. He was reticent when questioned, quietly smoking his cigarettes and sticking to the story of wanting to give the boys some excitement following the deaths of their father and uncle.

"We can only book him for kidnap." Said Will, "Yet I'm sure there is more to it. Hang onto him for a while. We have a few more hours before we have to let him go."

At lunchtime the phone rang. It was Dr Bray. The pathologist had found traces of Amanita Phalloides in Eddie's organs – death cap mushrooms!

"I must go to Beth at once." Said Dr Bray, a little too enthusiastically, Will thought.

"We've got him!" said Will to Graham.

He and a CID Detective went into interview Rick. He said little when faced with the results of the post mortem, then lit another cigarette, blew the smoke into three perfect rings and spoke:

"It would have worked you know. I studied the effects of the fungi. The early symptoms mimic an upset stomach, tremors and hypoglycaemia. This would have been the case if he had a stomach upset with his diabetes. So would the kidney and liver failure that occurred some 10 days after I administered the fatal dose. He loved his mushrooms, so I cooked him bacon, eggs and mushrooms one evening for supper after we had been drinking together in my cottage. George was easy, He was so damned predictable."

He lit one cigarette from the stub of another and continued:

"I knew when he went out that night that he would be legless when he eventually dragged himself out of the latest woman's bed. I just made sure the fluid was high in the dip trough, got a brick ready and waited. He never knew what hit him."

"But why kidnap the boys?" Asked Will.

"Ah! The boys! Well, they stood between me and the farm. I intended to make them disappear permanently, when Beth had got over her grief she and I could have...... 'It is not in the stars to hold our destiny, but in ourselves' .... well, I was prepared to wait, she would grow to love me as I do her, but that was the problem. You see, she loved the boys. They worshipped me. In the end I just couldn't do it. I honestly don't know what my next move would have been if you hadn't found us."

"You know what your short future holds now, don't you?" said Will. "The boys worship will turn to hatred of the man who killed their father."

Rick cast his eyes down, Will noticed slow tears running down his cheeks but he remained silent.

"What put you onto it?" Graham asked Will, as Rick was taken off to Wandsworth Prison.

"Well, you know the odd feeling in the pit of your stomach? Like Sergeant Watson got when he nabbed the Burmarsh sheep rustlers? I had that feeling and went to my old history teacher to find out about the York Brothers."

"Who?" said Graham.

Will continued: "King Edward 1V, he died from a mystery illness, possibly t

yphoid, but rumours of poison abounded. His brother, George, Duke of Clarence, had been drowned in a vat of Malmsey wine, leaving his two sons Edward V and Richard between his younger brother Richard and the throne. The crown prince and his brother disappeared, never to be seen again, some say on the orders of their uncle, who became King Richard 111."

Some months later Will was driving past the farm. The daffodils were just opening and the spring sunshine lifted the spirit. Dr Bray's car was outside the farmhouse. On a whim, Will pulled the steering wheel to the left and drove up to the house. Bella answered, she looked radiant, quite rosy cheeked and happy.

"Come in Sergeant. Have a coffee with us and share in the good news."

Will was ushered into the kitchen where Beth and Dr Bray were already seated round the big pine table with the coffee pot in front of them.

"Oh, Sergeant!" said Beth, breathlessly, "Dr Bray has asked me to marry him! We will wed in August so that the boys can be home for the wedding. The new farm manager is living in Rick's old cottage; he can keep the farm profitable for Edward when he is ready. Bella seems to get on well with him don't you Bella?"

Will noticed Bella flush, but she giggled like a schoolgirl and looked almost pretty.

Beth continued: “Edward will be going to the Agricultural College in Wye when he leaves school, but he and Richard will need Mr Neville’s advice on the farm for many years to come, so it seemed a good idea to employ him as manager - well Bella thinks so!“ (more blushes from Bella!)

As Will drove off he felt relieved that it had all worked out for the Whiteroses, They at least had a future as a family, unlike the York family of history. This reminded him: “I must take a bottle of something nice to Mr Gardener by way of thanks.“ He thought. “I always did enjoy the history lessons!”

Hero's return

My sister Edna was 14 when my parents bought her a darling little kitten for her birthday. He was black and white with a small black marking on his top lip that looked like a moustache.

"He looks like Hitler" My Mother told her.

"No! Absolutely not!" Shrieked Edna, with some force. This was 1940 and that gentleman had caused us great terror with nightly bombing raids on London, our home town.

"I shall call him Churchill." she chided with feeling, and so it was decided.

Now, despite the war, I was reasonably happy in my little world. True I missed my father, away fighting in India with the RAF, but my Mother, Edna and I were happy in our South London home. My Grandparents lived just around the corner and I had the usual friends and games to play; lots to occupy a ten year old girl. The only drawback was our next door neighbour Mrs Harris. She had always been nosey, gossiping to my mother about all and sundry, but lately she had taken to spying on my friends and I and reporting everything back to Mother. Edna said to be patient, she was just lonely and missing her husband who was away in the Navy. I was not so patient. Every Childish misdemeanour she instantly reported to my Mother and when I got home I would be grounded for a week and made to clean and lay the fires and fetch the coal from the cellar each day.

She copied us too. My Mother needed new kitchen curtains. The war was on and it was an era of make do and mend. Mother was very good with her needle. Sheets were sewn sides to middle when they got worn and collars were turned on blouses. The blue gingham curtains were worn and shabby and had shrunk over the years so that they gaped at the bottom. Mother took the lace hems from our old petticoats and sewed a hem on each curtain. This hid the worn end and lengthened them at the same time. The next week Mrs Harris had sewn white lace on each of her red gingham curtains.

Father came home on leave for a few days. We had a lovely time and Mother cried when he left for his train, but he was so shaken by all the air raids we endured that he persuaded my Mother to evacuate us all to the country. We went to a village in Devon called Landkey where we stayed with a lovely family called the Woodwards. They kindly allowed us to bring Churchill who was becoming quite a big cat. My Grandparents came too and, so did Mrs Harris although she was billeted close by! Most of the villagers were warm and welcoming to us but Mrs Harris soon got a name for herself as a busy body and a gossip. That Christmas it was decided to hold a communal village Christmas pudding making session in the church hall. My Grandmother remembered an old recipe from her childhood which utilised carrots and gravy browning to add richness of colour and some sweetness to the poor, wartime rations with which we had to produce our puddings. It went down very well with the villagers but Mrs Harris took the credit for this recipe.

Not long after we arrived in Landkey, my mother found that she was expecting a baby, my little brother Stephen. Mrs Harris made sure the village all knew about Mother's condition before she had even had the chance to write to my father.

"I don't know how she knows these things." complained Mother, "I haven't told anyone"

But I had seen Mrs Harris watch my Mother come from the Doctors house in the High Street.

The Woodwards were a wonderful help when Stephen was born but oh, how we all missed home.

Finally in May 1945 we were allowed back home to London. We left the beautiful Devon countryside and the lovely country people with great reluctance and went home. Luckily our house was still standing unlike some of our poor neighbours who were obliged to move into the new prefabs built hastily to house those whose homes had been bombed. The house next door was still standing so Mrs Harris moved back in and boasted the red gingham curtains as before.

Churchill, like the rest of us seemed to settle back into the old routine well, but one day he didn't come home. We weren't too worried at first but by the second morning Edna was beginning to fret.

"It's not like him, he always comes home for his breakfast." she wailed.

We searched the streets and all our friends searched high and low for him. Sadly to no avail. A street party was to be held in our road to celebrate the end of hostilities. On the Saturday of the party, about a week after the cat's disappearance, we were getting the tables laid and the bunting hung in readiness for the celebrations later that day. Edna had walked up to our Grandparents house to borrow a sheet to use as a tablecloth. She suddenly came running back waving her arms in excitement, her cheeks all flushed with happiness.

"Vi! Violet! Quick, tell Mum. Churchill's coming down Nan's road. He'll be here any minute."

I dropped the cutlery I was holding and ran to tell Mother. I could only have been in the house five minutes at most, but when we got back outside Mrs Harris had hung the Union Jack from her upstairs window and had gathered all the neighbours. They lined the street holding flags and craning their necks to see up the road. A slow smile played on mothers lips.

"Here he comes now!" she shouted.

A roar of cheering went up. Flags were waved madly and Mrs Harris curtseyed as, not our great leader, but our dear old black and white moggy strode around the corner, closely followed by an ecstatic Edna.

"That'll teach the old busybody!" whispered my mother, smiling to herself smugly.

The Sea Maiden

Ethan kicked a stone down the beach. It bounced and jumped until it landed on the sandy level strip, just before the water's edge. He watched as the foamy wave wet the dry stone, then he moodily kicked another with his hands thrust firmly into his trouser pockets.

He hated it when his daddy was away on the boat. He sometimes had to go away for days on these fishing trips and Ethan always wanted to go with him. Sadly he was only six years old and far too young to be a fisherman.

"One day," his daddy told him, "one day the Sally-Anna will be yours to sail and then you will be able to choose when to go to sea or stay but for now you must stay with nana and gramps and I'll see you in a few days."

Then kissing Ethan on the forehead his daddy grabbed his rucksack and left.

Ethan's mummy had died when he was just a few months old following a short but fatal illness. His father was a fisherman having inherited his own fishing smack from his own father. He employed a small crew. It made sense for Ethan and his father to move into the cottage by the harbour with Ethan's grandparents in the small West Country fishing port. This meant that when his father was on a fishing trip, Ethan was cared for and safe. He was a pupil at the small primary school, which he loved, but, the school was closed for the summer holidays until September, which was still four weeks away. His best friend, William, was on holiday with his mummy and daddy so Ethan was forced to play by himself on the small harbour beach within sight of nana's cottage.

He looked out to sea. Today was quite sunny and the sparkles of sunlight on the water made his eyes hurt with their brightness. He could see the seagulls wheeling overhead and, in the far distance, a bigger boat slowly moved across the horizon. Then he saw her. She was several hundred yards away; a lady with long golden hair. The sun highlighted it and made it shine as she swam towards a small cove just a few hundred yards from where Ethan was kicking stones. He hadn't been here before and it was just out of sight of nana's cottage. Today his curiosity had been aroused and it had made him daring. Who was she? He knew most of the locals and he hadn't noticed any holiday makers on the beach today.

Ethan crept up to the groin hiding the little cove. He knew he shouldn't leave the small strip outside his grandparent's cottage, and by NO means to go near the water, but he felt rebellious today. He looked guiltily up and down the beach and then cast a furtive glance at nana's cottage. All was quiet so he climbed over the groin and dropped down on the other side with a plop.

"Goodness you startled me!" The voice belonged to the lady he had seen swimming.

She was sitting propped against a rock by the entrance to a small shallow cave. Her legs were covered with towels and were invisible to him but, from the waist up, he could see that she was very beautiful and was brushing her long golden hair, made darker by the wetness of seawater. In her hand she held a small hand mirror. Ethan remembered the pictures in his story books at home.

"Who are you?" He asked.

"My name is Xanthe. And who are you?"

"I'm Ethan" he replied proudly.

He noticed the mirror and hairbrush. He also noticed that he couldn't see her legs. Daddy had read him stories of sailors that had met with mysterious creatures at sea. Mermaids were beautiful and, in his books, they always had mirrors and hair combs or brushes in their hands. Her name sounded alien to Ethan too.

"Are you a mermaid?" He asked. "I saw you swimming here a moment ago."

Xanthe looked amused. "Well now! I might be! But if I were I would hardly admit it to a mere mortal, now would I?"

Ethan's eyes grew wider and his mouth rounder. "Where are your legs?" he exclaimed.

Xanthe smiled. "Maybe I don't have any! That could be why I am such a good swimmer!"

Ethan was enthralled. He sat in the sand by her side and told her about his daddy and the Sally-Anna. He told how he always worried in case his daddy met a storm and didn't make it home safely and how he had no mummy. Xanthe was touched by the little boy. She promised that she would watch out for his daddy and the Sally-Anna and give it a mermaid's blessing; then she told him all about her coral home under the sea and her friends, the sea creatures and fishes. Finally, after a few minutes, Ethan heard his nana's worried voice calling him.

"I have to go now." He said. Then, on impulse, he threw his arms around her neck and hugged her. Xanthe kissed the top of his head.

"Bye Ethan, lovely talking to you and I will watch out for your daddy."

She waved as he climbed over the groin.

"Coming nana! Sorry I went out of sight."

He scampered up the beach towards his nana.

Xanthe's husband came round the corner of the cove a few minutes later with ice-creams.

"I had to walk miles for these!" he smiled as he handed her one. "When we've had these - if you are quite dried off - we'll head back to the car. The hotel will be serving lunch soon."

Xanthe smiled as she ate her ice-cream and told him about Ethan. Taking off the towels around the lower half of her body, she reached for the callipers to put on her legs, whilst her husband reached into the cave and unfolded her wheelchair before lifting her into it.

On the horizon the Sally-Anna was turning for home with a bumper catch.

The Lonely Garden

Letty looked at the house. 'A Victorian Pile' - that was how she had overheard her father describe it to her mother. This Victorian pile was to be her home for the next five weeks or so until the autumn school term began in September. Grey slabs of stone with the occasional pinkish hue to them, a plethora of chimneys on the slate roof and a long conservatory at the back of green wrought iron and glass panels; like a miniature crystal palace, her father jocularly told her.

Her father; he was the reason she was here. His job in the foreign office meant a transfer to Cairo for a year. Letty was just 15 and still at her private girls school near the Pomeroy London home in suburban Dulwich. She would stay in school as a boarder while her parents were abroad. This was a prospect she welcomed as she had many friends there and enjoyed her studies. The problem was that her parents had to leave just two weeks into the school summer recess. That was the reason Letty was coming to Devon to stay with her father's aunt Claris until school began again. The Housekeeper, Mrs Deacon showed them into the study where aunt Claris awaited them.

"Tea, I think, Mrs Deacon." she said.

"All in hand, of course!" answered the housekeeper, shaking her head, tutting and muttering under her breath as she left kitchen bound.

This amused Letty as she had rarely seen such cheek to a superior go unchecked.

Clarissa Pomeroy was a tall, thin lady of indeterminate age. Her hair, which was snow white and straight, was worn in a short bob. Letty noticed she was smartly but plainly dressed in a brown woollen skirt, pale green blouse buttoned right up to the neck. Lisle stockings and aggressive brogue shoes completed this ensemble. A small seed pearl necklace showed at the front under the collar of the blouse. This was the only decoration she wore. Letty noticed the room seemed to be stuck in the 1890's (some 35 years previously). Long sash windows overlooked the garden with distant views across the moor. The beams overhead looked gloomy and none too dust free (spider webs! - she suppressed a shudder). Her eyes took in the dark wood sideboard with the stuffed owl, mouse still in its beak, under a tall glass dome. An Epergne stood on the ancient piano containing white roses - the only things in the room that looked fresh and alive. The old long-case clock gave a comforting tick-tock in the background. Letty only had a minute to take all this in before her mother pushed her closer to Aunt Claris.

"Letitia, dear!" her Aunt said "Let's have a look at you!"

Letty noticed her aunt's very pale blue eyes had a twinkle and a small smile played around the corners of her lips.

"We will get along fine here together for a few weeks I am sure. You can help Mrs Deacon whenever you want, or, if that tiresome old curmudgeon drives you insane, there is always Brannigan, my gardener, he could always use a hand; or you could accompany me to the bookshop. I go there Tuesday, Thursday and Friday mornings to give Mr Blundell a break."

Letty looked at the large rug in the centre of the room - an expensive Persian, but old and threadbare in many places. The snowy white cloth on the tea table was fine Irish linen, but very thin and worn. She noted to herself that her aunt's work at the bookshop would help defray the considerable expense of keeping Coombe Manor and its staff of two together. Despite her scorn for her staff, Aunt Claris seemed fond of them and her blue eyes twinkled as she complained about Mrs Deacon. Tea was delicious with delicate sandwiches, cakes and pastries all cooked by the housekeeper and served on a very fine porcelain tea service. After tea Letty's parents made a move to go.

"Do you have to leave so soon?" whispered Letty to her mother; but her mother made soothing noises about her being fine, they had to get back to the hotel as they had long drive ahead the next day, still much packing to do and how they would write regularly. Then they were gone, driving out of the gates in the old Lagonda, with a final toot and a wave. Letty suddenly felt very young and alone.

"Come, my dear," said aunt Claris, "let's find your room, Brannigan will have put your things up there and I will help you unpack. We can then have a turn around the garden until supper when you can tell me all the things you like to do."

Letty's room was very pretty, a narrow bed with crisp white linen sheets and a pretty floral counterpane. It stood next to a corner washstand which contained a blue and white basin and ewer, a small bedside table stood the other side of the bed. A large chest of drawers and a huge wardrobe dominated the opposite wall, bookshelves stood above the bed, but Letty's eyes were drawn to the most exquisite rocking horse, dapple grey with an ashen mane and tail and red and gold saddle and reins. It was along the wall next to the door. Following her gaze aunt Claris said:

"Do you like him? I know you are too big for such things but it is so good to have a young person in Coombe manor again that I thought him wasted in the attic and got Brannigan to bring him down here. Mrs Deacon has given him a spring clean and spruce up for you".

Letty went to the long sash window; this too overlooked the garden but beyond the garden wall, just before the start of the Moor was another small walled garden, overgrown with weeds and devoid of ornament.

"That's an interesting little garden." Observed Letty to her aunt, "Why doesn't Brannigan keep it tidy like the rest of the garden?"

The Gardens at Coombe manor were a picture to behold, neatly manicured lawns and beautiful rich abundant flower beds, but this patch looked gloomy and neglected. To Letty's surprise her aunt looked serious and her lips tightened momentarily.

"We never use that part." she replied "In fact we keep the door from the main garden locked and bolted at all times. It's too much work for poor old Brannigan, no point in him tending it as I am happy with the gardens we do use. Come and see them."

With that her aunt took her arm and steered her downstairs for the pre-supper turn around the garden as promised. Letty got the distinct impression that her aunt had closed the subject of the lonely little garden once and for all.

The first few days were quite an adventure for Letty; she helped Mrs Deacon prepare the vegetables for lunch and supper and got some of the village gossip from her too. Brannigan let her help him in the orangery - not conservatory, as her father had said - when he tended the young plants and even showed her where to pick the vegetables for their dinner. Once she asked him about the lonely garden. It was only visible from her room upstairs as it lay in a dip and couldn't be seen from the drawing room or study windows.

"Missus don't like anyone going near the place, keeps the gate locked see! I don't even know if there is a key to it anymore; still! Less work for me and I got plenty of that anyways!" was all she could get from him.

A couple of times she went to the shop with her aunt to help. If anything it seemed more antiquated than Coombe manor, creaky uneven floors and dark shelves bowing with the weight of hundreds of musty old books. Her aunt sat behind a huge mahogany desk listening to an ancient wireless, waiting for customers and working on her embroidery. Letty helped to catalogue some of the books but, as she found it incredibly boring, she made her excuses after a couple of mornings. She stayed behind saying that she needed to keep up her studies. On one of these mornings she found herself flagging. It was raining; a fine constant drizzle that soaked everything. The Moor beyond the garden looked gloomy, misty and lowering and the sky an unbroken grey. She gazed out of the window as the clock inexorably ticked and a fat brown spider crawled across the windowpane and disappeared under the sash. From the drawing room the lonely garden was quite invisible as it was in a dip between the house and the moor. On impulse she ran up to her room, she could see it from there and she had an urge to see how gloomy and neglected it would look in the rain and mizzle. To her amazement, she found herself looking at the most beautiful garden she had ever seen. The lawn was green and as smooth as a croquet lawn, rose trellises abounded and a delightful sparkling fountain glittered in the sunshine. Sunshine! – Letty looked up at the sky, still grey with the relentless summer rain, but over the little garden it was dry and sunny. For a moment she was mystified, then the creak of the rocking horse drew her attention away from the window. He was slowly rocking as though a child had just jumped off him, when Letty looked back at the window, the garden was as overgrown as ever and the rain just as heavy there as everywhere else. Feeling a sudden panic grip her she ran headlong out of the room and rushed down to the kitchen.

"Mrs Deacon, Mrs Deacon!" she cried.

"Whatever is the matter, child, you look as white as a sheet!" Mrs Deacon was peeling potatoes in the kitchen. "Here sit down; you can roll out this pastry for me while I get you some lemonade you look like you've seen a ghost"

"Is the garden haunted?" Letty managed to ask, trying to sound matter of fact.

"Stuff and Nonsense!" said Mrs Deacon, "Who's been filling your head with rot? Brannigan I suppose, I'll have something to say to him, my lady!"

And she muttered on while Letty sipped the lemonade and waited for her nerves to calm.

A few days passed and Letty found she was quite enjoying her own company in the hours that her aunt was at the bookshop. When her aunt was there they held 'At Home' coffee mornings for the other ladies of the village, or visited them in return. The curate took them out in his old Morris to show Letty the beauty of the countryside and they picked and arranged flowers for the village church. But when she had time on her own Letty would gaze out of her window across the moor, or peer into the lonely little garden. On two more occasions she had seen it transform into what she guessed must be its former beauty, but only for a moment; and then it would once more become the overgrown neglected patch it was now. On more than one occasion she had walked into the room to find the rocking horse slowing down in motion as though a child had just jumped off its back. She had no explanation for either of these things, but each time she had felt in a dream-like state, only half there and not quite real. She put it down to her pining for her parents, being lonely, missing her friends and a dozen other excuses. She instinctively knew not to mention it to her aunt but could not quite think why. One night, about two weeks into her stay, Letty couldn't sleep; it was a hot sticky night, heavy with a bright full moon. Giving up on repose, she rolled over and opened her eyes. There on the horse rocking to and fro was a pretty blonde haired girl, of about eight years, smiling at her. Letty felt that she should have been afraid, but this girl did not look like a ghost. Golden ringlets framed her pretty face and she wore a pale pink dress from about forty years previously with a white organza apron over it. Long stockings and black button boots made up her outfit. She had blue ribbons holding her ringlets.

"Who are you? How did you get here?" asked Letty - more curious than afraid.

"I'm Emily. You are in my room and I want to show you the garden. It's my special garden but Mama says I cannot go there on my own. It's the moor, you see, bad people travel the moor; gypsies and sometimes convicts from Princetown. When the alarm sounds and a convict escapes, mama locks me up here to be safe."

They went to the window which was opened against the sultry night. By the light of the moon Letty could see the little garden. It looked beautiful by moonlight.

"Come on!" urged Emily, taking her hand and trying to climb onto the window ledge.

"What are you doing? Come away!" said Letty tearing her hand away from Emily's and stepping back into the room. As she did so lightning lit up the sky, there was a crack of thunder and the storm broke. Hard rain poured onto the dry cracked earth making dancing dollies on the ground. The garden had returned to normal. Emily had disappeared, and the air was decidedly fresher. Letty pulled the window to and went back to bed. She slept like a log for the rest of the night.

For some reason Letty felt she could not tell the others about Emily. She did ask Brannigan if a child had ever lived at Coombe Manor.

He gave her a sidelong glance and countered with "Why?"

Something in his face warned her off.

"Oh! Just the rocking horse, you know." she replied.

"Well now! I do know that one of your aunt's relatives had a child but she didn't live long and I'm not sure if she lived here at Coombe. Give me a hand with these gladioli will ye, standing around blethering all day!" and so the subject was changed.

The days drifted on as only days can, and Letty withdrew deeper into herself as she kept her own company. Many times she saw the garden transform and many times Emily would visit her. One day, a week or so before school was due to start again Emily came to Letty in the afternoon while she was in her room and her aunt was having her post prandial nap.

"Come with me to the garden." she begged Letty, "We have to keep it in its beauty. They neglect it!"

Taking Letty by the hand, she opened the sash. As if in a dream Letty climbed onto the sill.

"Hold my hand, we only have to step off! I just want us to play in the garden together."

Letty closed her eyes and prepared to step forward when:

"Miss, miss! For Pity's sake what are you doing?"

Brannigan's voice startled her back to reality. She fell back into the room just as Mrs Deacon burst through the door, she scooped a sobbing Letty into her arms.

"Hush there, child! Come down and tell Missus all about it."

Ten minutes later, while sipping hot strong tea, Letty heard all about it from aunt Claris.

"Your grandfather and I had another sister." Her aunt began. "Dorothea was a delicate soul prone to her nerves. She fell in love and married a soldier, John. They were very happy and had a daughter, a pretty little girl with blonde ringlets. They called her Emily. Not long after her birth John had to go off to fight in the Afghan campaign. Dorothea and the child moved back here while he was away fighting. Sadly he was killed and Emily became the apple of Dorothea's eye and her sole purpose in life. Dorothea was overprotective to her daughter; she was never allowed to play with other children in case she caught disease and became ill. Princetown is some miles away across the moor, but, when the siren signalled an escaped convict, Dorothea would not let Emily out of her sight and locked her in her room – your room – with her toys and rocking horse until the prisoner was captured again. Emily's one joy was the little garden. She loved to plant things and to play in there. One day, when Emily was about eight years old, the siren sounded. A convict had escaped. He gave them the run around this time and it was several days before he was found, dead on the moor. During that time Emily was locked in her room. It was summer time - warm nights and sunny days. The poor child spent hours looking out of her window at the garden. We think it must have turned her head because she jumped out of the window and was killed."

Letty shook her head.

Her aunt continued: "Poor Dorothea went slowly insane and had to spend the rest of her life in an institution for the mentally feeble. Tragic but it must have been in the family when you consider poor Emily's behaviour and now you!"

"No!" said Letty. "She was only trying to get out into her garden. She didn't mean to jump. She just thought she could step out into the garden."

Her face crumbled and she burst into floods of tears.

Over cups of tea and much weeping, Letty told her aunt of her experiences.

"The thing she would really love now - to give her peace - would be to restore her garden to its former beauty; like you did the rocking horse. Please!" She begged.

The Curate had offered to drive Letty and aunt Claris to the station for Letty's train back to school. As she left Mrs Deacon gave her a hug.

"See you at Christmas, Missy."

Letty could see Brannigan through the open gate in the garden wall. Her aunt had produced a key to the gate and Brannigan was making a start on clearing the weeds in the secret garden "See you in December, it'll be clearer by then, Miss." he said, waving.

The Curate waited in the Morris while Aunt Claris said Goodbye to Letty on the platform.

"I can't wait until Christmas to have you back again, my child." She said "Your Garden will be ready for the spring planting by then."

"Emily's garden!" corrected Letty, "And I can't thank you enough for having me, I am really looking forward to my return. I love it at Coombe Manor"

And she really meant it.

Out of this World

Miles stormed out of the house and slammed the door! Really Lucienne was becoming impossible; clearly this was the time to end it between them. When they had first met, she had seemed so delicate, rather fey and enchanting; fragile. Her white, porcelain like skin, jasper green eyes and long red hair had soon captivated him. She was so different from Penny, his domesticated little wifey back home. Making love with Lucy was exciting, out of this world, not like Penny. He always felt that it was something she endured as part of the wifely duties, totally predictable and routine!

Problem was, Lucy wanted more than just a fun time. She said she was in love with him and wanted him to leave Penny. How could he do that? Miles had made what his cronies at the golf club would say was a "good marriage". He had a lovely executive house on the new gated estate; he was chairman of the rotary club and treasurer of the golf club. Penny's father was an influential figure on the local council; He would face ruination if he left her. Penny came from a comfortable background; she had class and made a good impression on his arm at official functions. Lucy had nothing, living in a small terrace with her cats and joss sticks, meditating and living off her meagre earnings from her craftwork. If she was such a free spirit, why couldn't she just accept a fun relationship with no commitment? They must stop now that she was growing too needy, it was suffocating. He had told her as much that very afternoon while they got dressed before he left. The row had started when she asked him what time they would meet for the party her friends were having that night.

"Sorry babe, I can't make it. Penny has got her parents coming for dinner"

"Oh Miles, you PROMISED "whined Lucy "Why does she always have to come first? You say you love me, well when are you going to man up and leave her?"

So the row continued, getting more and more acrimonious until she threw her wineglass at him and it smashed on the wall behind his left ear.

"If I can't have you, she won't either!" she screamed.

"I pity you; you're pathetic" said Miles with a contemptuous smile and left, slamming her front door behind him.

It had been so convenient. Her cottage was in the same road as the golf course. That meant that twice a week he could take his golf clubs, tell Penny he was going to play a round (play around – good joke - nearly the truth he thought with much amusement), and go to Lucy. He always parked his car in the club car park so that if anyone saw it they could back up his story that he was at the club; a perfect arrangement. He glanced at his watch "God, is that the time" he thought, and ran the last few yards to the golf club, He was crossing the road to get through the entrance, but then, at the last second, he saw Lucy's old car come hurtling round the corner at breakneck speed, she had her arms rigid on the wheel, her eyes staring straight ahead. Miles froze for a split second, then just leapt back as she flashed past him, millimetres away. She was so close that he felt the rush of air whip past him. It spun him round. "Mad bitch" he thought to himself as he hurried on.

The house was strangely empty when he got in. No sign of an evening meal being prepared for their guests, and no sign of Penny. This was most unusual. He looked for a note in case she had needed to rush off to her parents, or something, but there was none. He went to the dresser to pour himself a drink, then thought better of it. Somehow he didn't feel like a drink this evening. He felt, suddenly, very tired, and flopped into the armchair. He must have dozed because the next thing he heard was Penny sobbing uncontrollably. Her father was leading her towards the couch holding her arm and a rather pretty policewoman was standing back, looking a little awkward.

"Pen, darling," he said, "whatever is it? What's wrong?"

He rushed towards her, but she blanked him as if he wasn't there

"George, what is it? What's happened?" he asked her father

"Officer?"

But they ignored him as if he didn't exist. He felt desperate now; he was shaking Penny's arm, but she seemed unaware of his presence. The policewoman was taking a call on her radio. He heard George say to Penny

"You can't stay here tonight, come back and stay with your mother and I until we have arranged the funeral at least."

Who's dead, Miles wondered. Why were they ignoring him? As Penny went upstairs to pack, her father turned to the policewoman.

"Why was he crossing the road there anyway? He was in the clubhouse, he shouldn't have been near the road"

"We don't know, sir." Said the policewoman. "They have just found a Morris Traveller parked up. They think it must have hit him. The driver had left the engine running and attached a hosepipe to the exhaust. They have taken her to Hospital but I'm afraid it doesn't look hopeful. We may never know what really happened, but it looks as though she was overwhelmed with guilt at killing Miles."

As he heard his name, Miles suddenly realised with sickening clarity why he felt so weary and why they were ignoring him. He was dead! The car hadn't missed him at all. Lucy had killed him. Bitch! What now, he thought, He looked frantically around, shouldn't there be a bright light, follow the light - isn't that what they say? He felt no different to usual, yet he was dead! What had he in store? Where was the golden light to take him up to his maker? That's what he had always read in the books, follow the light. He looked out of the window and saw Lucy approaching. He was somewhat surprised as he had just heard she was in hospital and in a bad way. She walked up his path bold as brass. Her usually pale face was flushed, cherry red, her lips were blueish. To his horror she walked straight through the front door which was closed fast at the time. He opened his mouth to scream but not a sound came from him. She smiled, then holding her pale finger to her blue-grey lips, she held out her hand. He felt a dread that made him recoil - yet he took her hand anyway. He was powerless to resist as she led him away towards... not the light, but a deep, black darkness, so black that the pressure hurt his ears. A thick blacker-than-black darkness

“Now we can be together for eternity! “ He heard her whisper “In everlasting darkness!”

The Day of Atonement

"I'm on my way, Graham." Will Simmons said, as he put the phone down.

Will had recently been promoted to Inspector and Graham Jessop had taken a promotion to Sergeant, both based at Lydd. There had been a terrible farming accident at a large arable farm on the outskirts of the village. One of the workers had fallen into the threshing machine and had been killed in a most horrific way. It appeared that the man had been working when he had slipped while standing by the wheels, and been dragged into it. The victim was identified as Tomas Hajek, a Czech national who had been working on the farm for the last year or so.

It would have been a straightforward accident except that, on close examination, remains of large pieces of wood were found in the machine; added to that, the farmer's wife, who had been outside in the yard feeding the hens, thought she saw a person run into the wooded copse at the bottom of the threshing field. At that point Graham decided that it was suspicious and called in Will. All the farm staff were questioned. No one knew much about Tomas Hajek. He kept himself to himself and made small talk only if his colleagues spoke to him. He was a morose sort of fellow, who always turned up and did his work thoroughly, was polite but did not seek out the company of his fellow workers nor ever mention his personal life.

"No one seemed to know him at all." Pointed out Graham to Will, "I doubt there is anything in it," said Will, "but we'd better make enquiries about the strange man seen by the farmer's wife. You talk to the staff; I'm going to the forensics lab."

Later that day they met up at the station.

"None of the staff saw anyone else near the machine at any time," said Graham, "but the postman just rang in to say he had noticed an old man limping out of woodland - the side the copse comes out onto. He thought nothing of it until he heard about the accident. "Well, it's an odd thing;" Will told him, "the Lab found traces of linseed oil on the splinters found inside the machine. That means it wasn't rough wood from the copse, but treated wood. Why was it in a threshing machine?"

Days past and there were no further clues as to what had caused Tomas to fall into the machine.

Will decided to attend his funeral. It was a sunny day but with a definite autumnal nip in the air. Looking around the ancient St Marys Church at Lydd, Will was saddened that there were only a handful of people present - the farmer and his wife and the curate. There was, of course, himself; plus an elderly couple, who sat at the back and tried to slip out, unnoticed, at the end of the service. But Will noticed them. And the old man had a slight limp. He hurried after them and soon overtook them. Introducing himself he asked how they came to know Tomas.

"We didn't" said the old man "but we, ourselves, are refugees from the Nazi oppression. I understand he was from Czechoslovakia. They were also under the yoke of the regime; we felt a bond with him."

"Do I detect another Czech accent?" asked Will.

The old man held out his hand; "Stanislav Krokosz and this is my wife, Irena. We are from Poland."

Will noticed the old lady was red eyed from weeping. Seeing his interest Stanislav added:

"She always cries at funerals, even the funeral of a stranger. She has very little English so please excuse her."

Will chatted to Stanislav, He was a stocksman at a neighbouring farm and he mainly worked with the horses. Even in 1957, some farms refused to give up the traditional farming methods. He had fled the Nazis in 1942 with his wife and niece. Being a Jewish family, from a small village outside Warsaw, they escaped the Nazis just in time. The rest of his family, including his niece's parents and brothers, were sent to the notorious Treblinka, along with most of their neighbours later that year.

"When the war finished there seemed little point in returning. Everything we had, and everybody we knew, had gone. We had made a life here, a good life. This is our home now."

Will thought about the local Polish community on his way back to the station. There were not many in Kent, but the few there were mostly worked on the farms. What had they been through in those war years he wondered? He had heard the stories of the extermination camps, the destruction of the ghettos, Nazi collaborators and the brave resistance fighters who opposed them. He had a "gut feeling" that the solution to this lay with the refugee community. He said as much to Graham the next morning while they drank their mid-morning tea.

"I think we should prod around a bit on the neighbouring farms"

Graham decided to start with the old couples niece.

Ewa Isdorczuk lived with her husband Marek on Summerside Farm, a huge egg farm where they both worked - living in a small pre-fab. They welcomed him into the tiny bungalow and made tea. Graham noticed Marek's ankle was strapped up and he was limping painfully.

"Ewa came here, with Stanislav and Irena, in '42. As you know." Marek told them. "I joined them in '45"

They seemed reluctant to talk about times in Poland. Not surprisingly, thought Graham, when most of your family has been wiped out. As he was leaving he showed them a photograph of Tomas Hajek. Ewa went very pale, and Graham noticed her hand shaking as she handed it to Marek.

"No," said Marek, "We don't know him – my wife is very squeamish. When she heard of the accident it upset her."

Graham wished them good day and left. As he got into the Police Wolseley, a small fair haired man came up to him.

"Hello, I'm Erik. Is Marek okay? Was it about his accident?"

Graham's normal reservation when dealing with gossip left him!

He said "Tell me your version of the events around the accident please."

Erik took a deep breath and began. It appeared that a week ago the monthly delivery of chicken feed arrived. Marek was loading it into the top granary using the pulley system when it snapped near the top dropping a 56lb bag of layers pellets onto Marek below. Erik's quick reaction – pushing him out of the way - saved Marek from serious injury or death. Marek had sprained his ankle as a result of the push. He put it down to ill fortune; but, on examination, Erik thought that the pulley rope had been partially cut. The farmer had not reported it. Thanking him, Graham left.

He and Will decided to find out what they could from Interpol about the Krokosz and Isdorczuk families and their associates.

Days passed and many farm workers were questioned from a wide geographical area. No one knew anything about Tomas Hajek. Then Interpol came back with some interesting news. Ewa Isdorczuk was not Stanislav's niece. She was born Ewa Lubetkin in a small suburb of Warsaw. Her parents had entrusted her to their closest friend and neighbours, Stanislav and Irena Krokosz, who had managed to smuggle her out of Poland in the nick of time. Her parents and brothers perished in Treblinka. Of Tomas Hajek they could find no record It was as if he had never existed!

Will and Graham drew up in the yard at Summerside farm. Before they could head to the prefab, Marek headed them off and drew them into one of the sheds.

"Ewa is out. This upsets her. Please talk to me."

Will told him of their discovery regarding Ewa's background. Marek looked deflated. "The Krokosz's have been very good to us. Stanislav is a good man - he cared for Ewa like a daughter. When he had the chance to escape, he sent Ewa and Irena ahead and stayed to fight the Nazis and the collaborators. It was a collaborator who betrayed Ewa's family, and mine, to the Nazis. Stanislav became a freedom fighter, tracking down and killing these traitors when he could. He was a brave man. He, and his comrades, organised the Treblinka uprising in '43; that is what enabled me to escape. I had seen awful horrors - enough to make a man insane. Almost a million of us were murdered in that camp between '42 and, when I escaped in '43. About 200 of us broke free. I was lucky and made it to Switzerland and safety. I heard afterwards that only about a quarter of us got away completely. The others..." (here he faltered, trembling; his eyes filled with tears) "the others were either killed or were forced to obliterate all signs of the tortures and horrors committed by the Nazi butchers!"

As they drove away Will told Graham to drive to the farm where Stanislav worked.

"I have some questions for that old man." he said.

Stanislav was not surprised to see them.

"Come into the parlour," he said, "we don't want to upset Irena."

Leaving her beside the fire in the kitchen, he led them through to the small, chilly, front room and motioned them to sit. Pulling up a chair from the dining table he began.

"I knew I had to do something when I saw which way the political winds were blowing in Poland. We had been herded into Warsaw itself - into ghetto's - it was obvious to me what the Nazis were planning. They always coveted our wealth, whilst despising us. Ewa was the young daughter of my best friend. She was never formally promised to my son, but it was an unspoken assumption that one day they would marry."

"Your son..." began Graham, but Will held up a hand to silence him.

Stanislav continued: "When things looked bad for us, I managed to get the women out of the country. I was not going to run like a hunted stag. I was prepared to die for my country and my faith. I went undercover."

Here he smiled, "I was the most feared freedom fighter those treacherous dogs had ever known! After the liberation, I came here. Ewa had met Marek - he is a good boy - they are happy and very much in love. The man responsible for our betrayal was in love with Ewa. He, too, came here looking for her. He called himself Tomas Hajek. Last week he tried to kill Marek. I know it was him! He wanted Ewa, and would not have given up until he had killed us all, except Ewa. She hated and feared him. I had to do something. I felt responsible for him, ashamed though I was of the treacherous dog!"

"What is Tomas' real name?" asked Will.

"Janusz Krokosz," said the old man, "and I wish I had never sired him!"

"It took him years to track us down - he was watching Marek and Ewa. It was him who cut the pulley rope injuring Marek. Next time he would have killed him. He was unaware that I knew he was here - his huge ego would not allow him to accept that; but nothing got past me. I found the farm he worked on easily enough. Nothing escapes the notice of the Polish community! Rumours of a Czech working in the area drew me to him. I saw him that morning, in the field working the thresher. It was fitting that I should choose that day. It was Yom Kippur - in our faith that means the Day of Atonement. We traditionally fast on this day. I find fasting sharpens the resolve and clears the mind. I crept unnoticed into the old shed at bottom field. There were some old farming implements, a few old toys, and, amongst the lumber, was a cricket bat. I took it and crept up behind him. He couldn't hear me with the thresher working. I had intended to strike him round the back of the head, but" (Stanislav paused and swallowed hard) "he was my son! I could not do it;

then I remembered my comrades, my neighbours, the life we used to have, and what he did in betraying us to the Nazis. I waited until he walked around the side of the machine, then threw the bat into the workings and ducked back round to the opposite side. The machine made a very different noise as it chewed up the bat. I knew he would check it. When he peered into the machine, I rushed him from behind and pushed him in. He never even knew I was there! He deserved it, I had sired a monster!"

Both Will and Graham felt compassion for Stanislav, and a degree of respect for his courage.

Will said, "You know you have to come with us now, don't you? Perhaps the court will take into account..." but the old man held up a hand to stop him.

"I know my duty!" he said. "Give me a minute with Irena."

As he disappeared into the kitchen Will said to Graham:

"Sometimes I really dislike this job - the law can be a stranger to justice."

They waited a few minutes then Will started to get a feeling of unease, Graham clearly felt the same, they looked at each other and at the same time they heard a dull thud coming from the kitchen. They ran into the room. Irena was slumped in the chair by the range, her face cherry red and darkening. Stanislav was still in the final throws of a seizure, he too had a red face but, in his hand, he held the remains of a broken glass phial.

They grabbed him but he stiffened and slumped - quite dead.

"Cyanide!" said Will. "The freedom fighters kept it against the chance of capture! Better death than give away their comrades under possible torture. Well, his tortures are over now, poor devil."

****

Early in spring Ewa and Marek came into the station to see Graham, He noticed that Ewa was expecting a baby, she looked radiant.

"We came to say goodbye, Sergeant. We found out that Stanislav and Irena had saved a small nest egg. They left it all to us. It is just enough to buy a small cottage in Lincolnshire. Marek has got a job working for an agricultural machine company as a salesman. The money is better, and the hours. We will need a little more space later!" She smiled and gently touched her swollen tummy.

Graham thought how pretty she looked. "I wish you all the luck and happiness for a bright future."